D0660673

When She's Your

Everything

By

Tina Marie

Tina Marie

When She's Your Everything

Copyright © 2016 Tina Marie

Published by Shan Presents

All Rights Reserved

www.shanpresents.com

This book is a work of fiction. Names, characters, places, and incidents either are the product of the author's imagination or are used fictitiously and are not to be construed as real. Any resemblance to actual persons, living or dead, business establishments, events, or locales, is entirely coincidental. No portion of this book may be used or reproduced in any manner whatsoever without written permission except in the case of brief quotations embodied in critical articles and reviews.

Acknowledgements

I would first like to thank God for giving me this gift of writing and for providing me with every blessing I have received this far and will receive in the future.

I want to thank my family, my fiancé Jay for putting up with all the late nights and my crazy moods when I was writing. To my kids Jashanti, Jaymarni and Jasheer I want you to know that I work so hard so you can have it all. I want to thank Shan for the opportunity to write with the best company out here and all of my pen sisters at Shan Presents for all of the love, support and for always helping to push me to my next goal, I appreciate you all.

To the crew, my sisters, Sharome, Shante, LaDora, Andrea and Taea I just want to say I love you all and without all the late night calls, test reads, brainstorming, word count challenges and mostly the friendship, without you guys there would be no book so I thank you all. When they see y'all they see me and that's how it is!! Nisey Jones I just have to say sis you are the best and I could not leave you out. I appreciate all of the late nights reading my work and giving me feedback.

To my friends and family, I appreciate all of the love and support. My cousin's Dionne & Tanisha. My friends Diana, Letitia, Natasha, Jade, Jennifer, Kia and Karen I am truly grateful for you all and I love you. Special shout out to Author Tiffany Forbes and the 50/50 club for providing an amazing platform for authors and readers to network. Authors Nek Hickmon, Shanice Swint, Jasmine and Chanique I cannot forget to thank you, I know you will all be best sellers soon. To all of my fans, readers, test readers and anyone who has ever read or purchased my work you are all appreciated and I promise to keep pushing on your behalf to write what you are looking for.

**Text Shan to 22828 to stay up to date with new releases,
sneak peeks, contest, and more...**
Check your spam if you don't receive an email thanking you for
signing up.

Text SPROMANCE to 22828 to stay up to date on new releases,
plus get information on contest, sneak peeks, and more!

Table of Contents

Chapter 1

Treajure

"Sasha, make me some breakfast please," I whined to my best friend who was already standing in the kitchen.

"Treajure, this is your house. Do you have no manners? You come make me something," she joked. I knew it was a joke because my ass can't boil water. Plus, I heard her moving the pots and pans around, getting ready to make something. Looking at the kids jumping up and down and clapping their tiny hands, I bet they were happy I wasn't cooking, too. Throwing myself on the couch with my IPhone in my hand, I began scrolling through my timeline, liking stupid memes and videos. I should probably be studying. I'm in school for International Business Law, and there is always stuff to remember and read. But today, I felt like relaxing. We had a three-day weekend and I was looking forward to going out tonight and enjoying myself. I hadn't been to a club in almost a year because my school program is competitive and comes with a lot to keep me busy. Plus, I have two and half-year-old twins who keep me running.

Watching my nephew Kaneil Jr. and my twins Janai and Jyion Jr., or JJ as we call him, play with their zillions of toys with one eye half-opened, I could feel myself start to drowse. My phone fell next to me and the constant buzzing told me it was probably annoying ass Lamar, but this little nap was feeling so good I couldn't take the time out to look.

Lamar was this guy I'm talking to, and his ass is special, and not in a good way. Ignoring the phone, I rolled over to get into this good nap until my food was ready. But as soon as I did, the doorbell began to ring. Hopping up with a smile, I ran to the door.

"JJ it's auntie Nevaeh at the door," I told my son because he was in love with my friend Nevaeh. As soon as I opened the door my smile turned right the fuck upside down.

"What the fuck Treajure, you don't see me calling you? And who the fuck told your hot ass to come to the door in those skimpy ass shorts and a bra on," he began berating me like I was his child.

I was still shocked at how this motherfucker thought it was ok to just drop by my house unannounced when I'd never invited him to come for a visit, or come in on any previous occasion. I don't bring random men around my kids, hell their own daddy had never even seen them, so I needed him to have several seats and move from in front of my house. Before I spoke I chose my words carefully as I shooed the kids away from the door with my hand. Turning back to face Lamar, I took a deep breath before I began.

When She's Your Everything

"Lamar, let's start with why you have showed up to my damn house unannounced, no phone call or nothing? You know I have kids and you have not met them, so don't be popping your yellow ass over here talking shit to me. And second motherfucker, this is a half shirt, not a bra and I was in my house in my pajama's laying down before you decided to bother me," I told him firmly trying not to cuss his annoying ass out in front of my neighbors.

"Hey girl, you got me fucked up. I'm your man and will come to this motherfucker anytime I want to. You rude as shit not inviting me in or nothing. Those kids are like my damn kids since I am wit' you, so they gonna have to get used to me being around, and so are you," Lamar yelled, roughly grabbing my arm. Not even giving him a chance to get a good grip I kicked him in the knee and jumped back. Shit I was aiming for his balls.

"Lamar, you don't own me. We talk, that's it. I'm not your wife or wifey. And furthermore, you don't pay the fucking rent here."

His mouth popped opened to respond, but another voice beat him to it.

"You damn sure don't pay shit up in here. I do," Covey said as he strolled up the walkway with his hand on his waist.

I already knew he was going for his gun. But, I could also see all my nosey ass neighbors watching the scene unfold right before they eyes, like this was a fucking IMax show. Even the good areas are filled with busybodies that don't work or have shit else to do but watch you. Miss Sanchez was hanging out the window so far her head scarf fell off and landed on a bush. Shit, I almost laughed out loud as she hurried and popped her hand up to grab her wig before it fell too. Instead, I snorted and tried to focus on the issue in front of me, before Lamar ended up with a bullet in his head and I had to clean the blood off the steps, which was not in my plans for today.

"Hey big head, what brings you to town?" I cheerfully called out to Covey, trying to lighten up the situation. "This is my friend Lamar. Lamar this was my brother's best friend, Covey. Lamar we're having a family day, so I will call you later before I go out," I said as I rushed Covey in the house and Lamar off the steps. "Babe, I'll walk you to the car because I'm sure Sasha wants to catch up with her brother anyway."

I could see his ass mumbling to himself. As long as he knew what was good for him and kept that shit to himself, we're Gucci. As soon as Lamar was on his way, Nevaeh came walking up from the bus stop at the corner.

"Hey girl, why didn't you call us for a ride? No one wants to be taking the damn bus." I fussed at my friend while giving her a hug.

"It's cool, Trea. I was only up the road anyway. Now move so I can see my future husband, Mr. JJ."

She almost knocked me down running to drop to her knees and grabbed JJ in a bear hug, causing him to squeal and laugh in joy. This why I keep my circle small. Me and Sasha have been friend since we were four, and when we came to America and started college, we met Nevaeh and she just fit right in. I need my friends to be people my kids love and want to be around, we're like a family. Seeing her stare at Covey with questions in her eyes and a little lust, I figured I should introduce them, since Sasha's ass didn't. Even though I know Nevaeh had a man, there ain't shit wrong wit' upgrading and Covey is definitely an upgrade from a lot of niggas.

"Covey, this is our friend Nevaeh. Nevaeh, this is Sasha's older brother, Covey. Well, he's is like my older brother too. A bossy, crazy, mean ass older brother," I said joking. Shit, Covey is the one who made sure we even came to America and financially, he takes care of everything for us. At first I wondered for a long time how my mother was able to save enough money to send me to my aunt in Brooklyn, but later I found out Covey was the one who gave her the money to send me, and once he came here, he made sure me and the twins were straight.

"It's nice to meet you," she said in a quiet voice with a slight blush rising up her neck to her cheeks. Nevaeh is normally soft-spoken so I wasn't surprised that she was over there acting all shy and shit. I guess she couldn't resist Covey's looks; he is cute, but his attitude, uh uh.

Seeing Covey narrow his eyes, I knew he was about to be ignorant as fuck. And, just like that, before I could stop him, he opened his mouth and began to speak.

"I don't really care about meeting you, so stop looking at me like I am your last fucking meal. Shit, where you find her at? She looks like a thot," he said, then went to sit on the couch and turn the channel on my TV.

"Covey, how the fuck she look like a thot? She got a sign on her forehead or something?" I asked him with shock in my voice. He had his moments, but damn he was taking it too far. My friend was a nice girl and she doesn't bother anybody.

"Sis, see how her ass jiggle in those tights when she bend over? That's the thot jiggle. Hell, I don't even think she has on panties in those tight ass pants. Yo' can your pussy breathe in that shit? I think it's being suffocated?" he began laughing at his own questions, not really expecting an answer.

Before I could even scream at him, Nevaeh just rolled her eyes and mumbled, "fuck nigga," before she walked into the kitchen. Well damn, so much for playing matchmaker wit' these two crazy mo fo's. I hope he ain't hurt my girl feelings; he was being a fucking hater since I know she looked good as fuck. I don't have bummy looking chicks in my circle. Looking at Covey holding Janai in the air up towards the light, inspecting her like she was an alien or an exotic bug, I wondered what he was going to say next. I hope he didn't realize who the twins' dad was. Trying to avoid his eyes when he caught me looking, I could feel the sweat trickling down neck.

"So Treajure, when was you going to tell anyone that these kids belonged to my cousin? Or you was just gonna let them grow up with no dad or nothing. Damn, you hate him that much you would keep his kids from him? I just don't understand what the fuck happened between you two. Y'all asses used to be inseparable," he said, shaking his head and looking sad. He was making me feel like shit. But I had to do what was best for me, and considering the last time I told Jyion I was pregnant our baby ended up dead, I wasn't taking any chances.

Seeing Sasha slither her way to the stairs, I knew I was going to have to face the music alone.

"Covey look, I will tell him when the time is right, and honestly I don't even know where the hell he is at. I tried to call him once I had the twins, and he hung up in my face. When they turned one I tried again, and the number was cut off," I pleaded my case, but I knew most of it was bullshit since I'm sure Covey or even Sasha have contact with him.

"Trea, you know you sound whack as fuck right now. I'mma let you have that. But let me tell you something, you better fix this shit before it catches up to you. And Sasha, I know your ass knew too, so stop hiding upstairs. No telling what the fuck else you up to. I know it ain't just Trea's ass on some bullshit today. Anyway, I just came to tell you both I am going to be in town for a while. I'm tired of the city. Plus, I can see the two of you on some bullshit so I'mma have to become more involved in what's going on around here." Throwing two stacks of money on the table, he got up to leave. "That's for you guys to buy the kids some clothes. Shit, all this money I been spending to take care of these little big head babies and they belong to Jyion ass all along. I'm about to start taking this shit right outta this nigga cut from now on. Oh yea and Treajure, tell that nigga Lamar I'mma see his ass in the streets."

Giving us hugs he made his way to the door. "Later, thot," he called out to Nevaeh, winking at her as the door closed behind him.

Hearing Nevaeh laugh, we all fell out on the floor laughing hard as fuck. That nigga Covey's always been wild as hell, and had no filter on the shit that he said or did. I'm happy he's in town but kinda sad at the same time, because I know he's gonna be watching everything we did and clearly offend our friends and shit.

"Sasha, you remember when your mom asked all the kids if she looked like a maid and Covey's bad ass was like yes? Man, she took the broom and beat the mess outta him. Nevaeh girl, please don't take his ass serious. He's just one of those niggas, always miserable and talking shit. His mouth is a mess and has been as long as I can remember."

"Girl it's ok. Too bad, because he is fine though. Maybe he just need some good pussy to give him some act right," she said with a big goofy smile on her face. I just shook my head and grabbed my plate of food. I could see Covey had met his match. Usually, females cry when he's finished fucking wit' them or at least look sad, but not my girl. She was ready to fuck him into submission.

Chapter 2

Sasha

Damn, I'm not feeling my brother being in town at all. Don't get me wrong, I love the shit out of my older brother. Covey sacrificed a lot for me and my son, and for Treajure too. He hit the streets hard after Kaneil was killed, and made sure me and Treajure got out of Jamaica and off to college and a *better life*. Shit, I still wonder exactly what he does to make money. I guess any and everything. It works, because he's made sure we had a place to live and food to eat, and I ain't miss a meal yet. He's the best big brother. Especially when he is in Brooklyn doing his own thing, and Trea and I are down here doing ours. Seeing how pissed he was about Lamar made me scared as fuck for him to find out who I am messing with. I guess that's why Ajay told me not to mention to anyone in my family that we're messing around. I hope he knows my brother and cousin will kill him if he hurts me.

Looking through my clothes in my overnight bag for something to wear to the party, I found two outfits I wanted to try on. The first one was a light blue short romper that clung to my body like a second skin. Twirling around in the mirror, I liked it, but decided to give outfit number two a chance. As soon as I pulled the black shirt dress over my head, I knew I was wearing this outfit instead of the romper. It flared out right before my knees and made my legs look long and sexy. The gold accessories I put on made the outfit pop. Throwing the clothes on the bed, I put my purple workout shorts and a white and purple sports bra on. I decided to lie down since everyone else in the house was taking a nap. The twins where laying with Nevaeh and KJ was with Treajure. He's very close to his auntie. Anytime they are around each other, he wouldn't leave her side. I am glad they have that relationship. Especially since that is all she has left of her brother.

Before I could even get my eyes closed, my phone was going off with Ajay's ringtone. He always called at the worst times. But I knew if I didn't answer him, I would spend the whole rest of the day and evening arguing with him about why I missed the call and what I was "really" doing. This relationship was beginning to feel like a prison and he was the warden. Making sure he heard the sleepiness in my voice, I answered the call.

"Hello Ajay".

"Sasha, why the fuck the phone rang so many times when I called you? What the fuck is your sneaky ass doing?" he began questioning me at hello. Now I felt like I had to defend myself to him, even though I wasn't doing shit but lying around my people's house about to take a nap.

In an annoyed tone I responded, "Ajay, I wasn't about to do shit but take a nap while KJ is taking his."

"See Sasha, that's the shit I'm talking about. You have a big fucking attitude when I ask you some shit. Every time you get around that whore ass friend of yours Treajure, you start smelling yourself, and I am tired of it."

He went on and on with the nonsense for so long Kaneil Jr. came in my room to tell me he was ready to go to Auntie Fi's house. "SASHA, are you even fucking paying attention to what I'm saying to you? This bitch Siri called me a nigga today! I am fucking Apple up. I ask this bitch for an address and when she gave it to me she called me a bitch nigga. I knew these Apple motherfuckers was prejudice as hell."

I had to put the phone down and laugh into the pillow. I was laughing so hard my belly was hurting. Yea, I programmed this dummy's phone to call him a bitch nigga. He called himself hiding the little black dress I was wearing tonight, so I got pissed and decided to fuck with him. *Bitch nigga.*

Picking the phone up to hear him calling Siri a bitch and her asking him to not use profanity, I stifled my laughter so I could get him off my line and get ready to go out.

"Babe look, I have to go and get the baby ready to take to my aunt's. I'mma make you feel better when I come over tomorrow. Oh yea, and don't ever fucking call my best friend, my sister, a whore. If you do, I will cut your shit off and throw it in the river. Later." I hung up without waiting on a response.

I know it's like why the hell do I even mess with Ajay if he gets on my nerves so much. I honestly don't even know why I started talking to him. It was like a sign when I saw him here after I first came to New York. KJ was a baby and I was in Walmart pushing the cart when, out of nowhere, Ajay just popped up and called my name. I was so happy to see someone I knew, because the only person I had in Rochester was my Aunt Fi. This was before Treajure came from NYC, so I was so lonely and still trying to get over the death of Kaneil. I used to just talk to Ajay for company. Sometimes he would take me out to eat or to a movie, and always seemed to be wherever I was. Like, any party I would go to, he was there too. After about two years of him begging me to date him, and to be his woman so he could take care of me, I finally just said ok. Since I knew in my heart I couldn't fall in love with another man after Kaneil, I just decided to be with Ajay.

As soon as I got dressed, I went to check on everyone else. I always got ready first because I had to fix their hair and make-up. That was my specialty and I loved making people look good. I wanted to have my own exclusive beauty salon one day, but for now I have a chair in my cousin Ray's shop.

"Excuse me Nevaeh, who you looking so hot for tonight, miss? I wonder is it because Covey is going to be there," I teased Nevaeh as I finished her makeup and spun her around in the desk chair. I was playing with her, but also for real. Usually, Nevaeh goes out in some jeans and a t-shirt and rarely lets me do any make up.

"Alright, ready. Let's go now, because we're always late and I don't want to stand in line," I fussed as I led the way to the door. I grabbed JJ and his bag, knowing that everyone else would follow.

My aunt only lived around the corner from Treajure, so dropping off the kids didn't take long. Climbing back into my all-white 2015 BMW, I could feel the butterflies in my belly. I hoped Treajure didn't hate me by the end of the night. I knew that my cousin was in town too, and was going to be at the club tonight. I didn't want to be in the middle of their drama, so I never said anything. Plus, I know if I would've told her, she would've stayed her ass at home. She is stubborn and has to face him sooner than later because where we live is small so better they just get it over with before she bumps into him by surprise.

As soon as I reached downtown, I was already in a bad mood. Ajay had texted me a bunch of stupid shit, calling me a cheater and claiming I was out looking for a man tonight. He was saying that he didn't care if my brother was visiting; he knew what I was really up to. I was so tired of him, and to top it off, I'd circled the block three times and couldn't find parking. Kissing my teeth, I finally decided to just pull up to valet parking. I wasn't big on patience and my heels were too cute to be walking far.

"Sasha, I hope you going to dance tonight, because I don't want to be the only one out here showing off," Treajure said to me.

Laughing, I walked to the VIP door of Water Street and walked in the club.

As soon as we headed upstairs, I saw the look of surprise on Treajure's and Jyion's faces. Smirking at Covey to let him know I saw him watching my friend, I began looking around the private tables they had in our section, and that is when I saw him. He was sitting in a chair in the corner, drinking something out of a cup. His dark eyes looked serious, as always. He had on a white Polo shirt and white cut-off jean shorts that complimented his light brown skin. He wasn't light-skinned, but the color of peanut butter. His good hair was cut kinda low, but it was still long enough for me to reach out and touch. It was dark like coal, and looked soft like baby hair. I could see the cut on his eye from when he had a run-in with the police as a kid and they took a machete and chopped him in the face.

I still remembered watching the blood drip down his face as he ran away from the police, still holding the tin of corned beef he stole from the shop in one hand. I ran after him until we got close to the scheme we lived in. He didn't go to his house. Instead, he sat on a huge rock, took out his knife, and cut the can open. He started eating it just like that. It wasn't cooked and blood from the cut was all over his face, but I could tell he was hungry. I took off my sweater and held it up to his face. He didn't say a word, just dropped his head in pain. That was the day me and Tavian became friends.

Seeing that his watch, earrings, bracelet and chain were all shining in the club lights let me know that Tavian came a long way from the how he grew up. He didn't smile, but I could see the smile in his eyes when he looked at me. Motioning for me to come over, I slowly walked to where he was sitting. I felt like I was in a fog. My head was spinning and I almost tripped walking to the table. *Shit, I need to get it together. It's just Tav, and I don't know why I am acting like an idiot.*

"Sasha, you looking good, it has been a long time," he said as he got up to hug me. I didn't want the hug to end, and for the first time in years, I felt excitement from a man's touch who wasn't my dead boyfriend. The only problem was Tavian was my dead boyfriend's friend.

"Hey Tavian, you're not looking bad either. Where is your girl at, while I'm over here hugging you and shit. I don't want anyone jumping out the shadows trying to ruin my cute outfit," I joked with him, even though I was kinda serious. Niggas who were well-dressed usually have a female picking out their shit.

"Well damn Sasha, hello to you too. Who said I had a girlfriend? I'm single, unless you want the job," he responded with a half-smile.

Feeling someone's eyes on me, I turned slightly to see Ajay burning a hole in my back and staring at me with an evil look. Realizing that Tavian had my hand in his, I snatched it away quickly and decided it was time to end this conversation ASAP.

"Alright Tavian, it was good to see you, but my man is giving me the evil eye so I have to go."

Tavian looked up and straight at Ajay before snatching my phone, calling himself, and smirking at the same time. Putting the phone back in my hand, he gave me one more hug. As he pulled me close, I could feel the gun on his waist. Shit, I wasn't surprised one bit. He'd always been about that life. He made sure to kiss the side of my neck in the process. Damn he was turning me on big time, I don't know what was hotter the kiss or the fact he just didn't give a fuck about Ajay standing right there. "Aight Sasha you want me to walk you over there or you good?" He asked. Waving at him I walked away as fast as I could, I know how Tavian gets down and as much as Ajay pisses me off I don't want him dead, at least not today.

Chapter 3

Treajure

Walking in the club, I felt like the shit. I'd been ignoring Lamar's ass ever since earlier when I made him leave my house. Then he had the nerve to be mad. I saved his punk ass life. But whatever, you can't tell these niggas nothing these days. Checking myself in the reflection of the mirrors placed by the doorway, I was happy with what I saw. My hazel eyes stood out in the light. My dark brown skin was glistening against the all-white romper I had on. My curly hair was pulled up in a ponytail and held together with a diamond looking clip that matched my necklace and earrings. To top it off, I had on a pair of deep pink heels from Aldo that matched the pink of my lipstick.

Following Sasha as she led the way, I was feeling myself, dancing and snaking my body, just showing off because I could. I remembered a time when I was younger, I used to think I was ugly.

Mainly because my brother was so fucking pretty I would feel like I couldn't compare. Now, I *know* I am the baddest bitch when I walk through the place.

Looking at my friends, I smiled because all eyes were on us. Sasha was wearing the hell out of this tiny ass dress that was all black. It just flowed out like a shirt almost, and she had matching gold accessories and shoes. Her light skin was sparkling with the Victoria's Secret lotion with the sparkle shit in it, and her short hair was laid in a perfect bob. I knew Covey was gonna kick her ass with that shit she had on, and I was going to be happy she was in trouble and not me this time.

Neveah, who was usually quiet and a plane Jane, dressed up and showed out tonight. I wonder if it was because I told her Covey's was going to be here. Shit, she did have a man. But I had yet to meet Frank, even though they live together and she'd been with him since before I met her. He never came with her to do shit and I personally didn't think he was very nice to her, based on some of the phone conversations I had heard. But I try to be that friend who minds her own business and shit.

Anyway, it would be his loss if he kept it up, because when Nev pulled herself together, I mean whoa. She had on a peach-colored skater dress with the back out and a pair of silver heels to match her silver accessories. Her long sew-in was all the way down her back with some spiral curls at the end. Her almond-shaped eyes where brought out by the little make up that she had on. When she walked, her ass sat up and just bounced. Looking around, I saw Covey wave us upstairs to VIP, and his eyes were all over Nevaeh's ass. His and every other man's in the place. She had to give a dozen men rude stares and flip them the bird as she walked by and they reached out to cop a feel or just slap her ass.

As soon as my foot hit the top step to VIP, I felt like someone had punched me in the fucking throat. There he was, standing across the room, a Guinness in one hand and leaning against the bar without a care in the world. Until he caught my eye. I couldn't believe I was looking at Jyion after three years. He still looked almost the same as the last time I saw him, except the little twists he once had were now almost dreads that he had pulled up in a ponytail on his head. Watching him walk over to me quickly, my heart began to race. Here was the man I loved but I hated, making his way over to me after all of this time. I honestly thought I would never see him again. I hoped I wouldn't, because these feelings were too much to deal with.

Before I knew it, his six-foot frame was towering over me. He was so close I could smell his Armani Code cologne, making me want to snuggle into his arms and live there.

"Jyion, it's nice to see you, as always. I see life has been good," I said nervously, hoping he would back up, a lot. Instead, he moved closer. His jeans were rubbing up against my bare legs and his arms had me trapped against the wall. He was so close, his iced out Jesus chain dipped inside my romper and was touching my bare breasts. Leaning his head next to mine, he kissed my cheek.

"Treajure, I missed you. I can't believe you stayed away from me this long," he said in his thick accent. Damn, how could I forget how sexy he was? How much he turned me on just by breathing next to me? "So I heard you had a baby, yo. What the fuck is that about? I hope you know that nigga who breed you is a dead man."

Hearing him mention the twins, I panicked and began shoving my way past him. I had to get away from him for a few reasons. One, I'm scared to tell him about the twins, and two, I was scared of the deep feelings I still had for him. Seeing him brought me back to all the days we spent time together, all the years I spent having a crush on him when he was hanging out with my brother. Feeling him come up behind me as I stood over the balcony of the VIP looking down, I didn't know what to do. This time, he didn't say anything. He just pulled my body closer to his, and I began moving a little to the music. It was just like old times. I kept trying to look around, hoping no one noticed me and him, because I knew Lamar had a lot of friends. And this was crossing the line since I was dating him, even if I kinda didn't want to be.

A lot of people came to talk to him, but he never left my side. Looking over at Sasha with a "help me" look on my face, I could see her looking pissed off about something and not paying me any attention. Seeing Lamar walk through the front door and start looking around, I knew he was trying to find me. I felt Jyion's dick poking me in the ass, I knew I had to get away from this nigga, and quick. I thought about lying and saying I needed to use the bathroom, or that

Sasha and Nevaeh needed me. But fuck it, he was gonna find out I had a man soon enough.

"Look Jyion, I'm trying to be nice and move away, but you not getting the hint. I have a man and he just walked in, so I need you to back up," I said, while once again moving away from him.

"Oh yea, you got a man huh? I guess it's that pussy ass nigga Lamar, right? Is he the one who you got a baby wit'? Yo, I'mma let you go, for now," he said, running his hand down my arm, making me shiver, then laughing as he walked off.

He was laughing so hard his drink was spilling all over the place. Feeling depressed to see Lamar, I figured I would go downstairs and meet him so he didn't run into Covey again. Especially with Jyion and Tavian here. Those three together had no damn sense, especially Tavian. He still looks like the killer he was when we were kids, and I didn't think these dudes realized yet that in America you can't just casually kill people like back home.

Grabbing Nevaeh by the arm, I whispered in her ear, "Come with me so I don't have to deal with Lamar alone."

"Girl, if you don't like his weird ass, then why do you mess with him?" she said with her pretty face twisted into a frown.

"Why you always calling Lamar weird?" I asked.

She shrugged her shoulders and was about to speak, when a pretty light skin chick with Goddess braids bumped her so hard her drink spilled all over the floor. Seeing the girl look back and smirk, I knew it was about to be some shit.

"Hey Tauni, what's your fucking problem? Oh, I know. You can't keep a man, right bitch?"

Nevaeh never said another word, just grabbed the girl by her thick braids and punched her in the face several times until blood spewed everywhere. That was when I saw her ugly ass friend come up on the left looking like she wanted to jump in. This bitch had some straight backs, baggie jeans, and a white tee on like she was a man. If it wasn't for the girly face and big breasts, I wouldn't have been able to tell the difference. Before she could even make a move, I used the keys on my key ring to cut the red bull can I had in my hand in half. Using the jagged edges, I sent them into her body a few times. I felt strong arms around me, pulling me away and picking me up. Before you knew it, I was almost out the door.

Watching Covey grab Nevaeh as we all headed out the side door, I looked around for Sasha. Finally spotting her, it looked like she was talking to that nigga Ajay from back home. I didn't know he lived here, and that she and him were cool. I didn't like that nigga one bit. There was something about him that made my skin crawl. He used to always watch me like some weirdo when we were younger. Not just sometimes, but every time he saw me, he would just stare with a retarded face.

She was so close to him she was almost in his lap, and it looked like they were arguing about something. At the last minute, she ran with her heels in her hand to catch up to us as we left before the cops came. As my baby's father was dragging me out the door, I could see

Lamar with a really pissed off look. He was so mad his whole face was turning bright red as he watched me from the bar. Shit. Realizing I'd ended up in the car with Jyion, all I could think was it's going to be a long night.

"Yo, where you live so I can take you home? And since when you start cutting chicks in the club and shit? That's not you, Treajure. You're not a thug," he lectured with laughter in his voice. "Ma, that bad girl shit turns a nigga on," he added, grabbing his dick that was rock hard in his jeans. He was distracting me even further and I almost slipped and gave him my address. At the last minute, I realized he couldn't know where I lived or come in my house. The second he saw the twins or a picture of them, he would know they were his.

"Just take me to Sasha's house. We're all staying there tonight."

Taking out my phone and texting the girls after rejecting three calls back to back from Lamar, I let them know what is going on so I we could all go to the same place.

When he pulled up to the house, I jumped out so fast I tripped on the curb and fell to the ground.

"Damm Trea, you running from me or you drunk?" Jyion called out from above me as he held out his hand to help me up. As soon as his hand touched mine, I felt chills run through my body.

Walking through the front door, the house was quiet, but since Sasha's car was parked I guessed her and Navaeh had already gone to bed. I headed to the kitchen to grab a water and some Tylenol because I already have a headache and the way Lamar keeps calling my phone I can tell it will be worse sooner than later. "Ok Jyion we are all home safe now, you can go back to your hotel or wherever you are staying." I told him trying to get him to remove himself from my space.

Instead of leaving, he came closer, just staring at me. I tugged on the shorts of my white romper, feeling self-conscious all of the sudden with this little ass outfit I had on. Hearing my phone ring again, I decided answering Lamar might make Jyion leave.

"Hey babes whats up?" I answered in a sexy voice. I was trying to make it seem like I was in love with my man so this nigga would back off of me a little. "What the hell is going on Treajure? I've been calling you for the last forty minutes, and who is that tall ass nigga who was carrying you out of the club? Let me guess, another one of your dead brother's friends? You know what? You need to get your ass to my house now, because I know you ain't home and you not gonna be out here playing me like some punk ass nigga."

"Lamar look, I'm at my best friend's house and already in for the night. Plus, you know I'm not driving, so I will be to you as soon as I wake up and someone can take me to get my car." I was trying to keep my voice at a level tone so Jyion couldn't see how annoyed I was, but it didn't even matter. Lamar starting yelling, and Jyion came over and snatched the phone.

"Jy, give me fucking phone," was the last thing I got out before he hung up on Lamar and snatched me closer to him. I would be a liar if I said my pussy wasn't wet. Shit, she felt like she was trying to jump out of my romper and into his pants. Trying to speak, all I got out was a moan as his lips sucked on my neck.

"Ahhh, damn baby, you like that don't you. I know you miss this dick," he talked shit as he pulled my romper and panties to the side, ripping my thong in the process.

Feeling the head of his dick throbbing against my clit made me cum instantly. I sat on the top of the counter, shaking, waiting for more. As soon as I felt him enter me, I tensed up. I swear he was bigger than I remembered, and definitely bigger than Lamar. Just like that, Jyion was fucking the shit out of me in Sasha's kitchen. I think I came like four times before I felt his dick jerk inside of me. I knew he'd done the worst possible thing and came in my pussy. As soon as he let me down, I hung my head in shame and ran upstairs. I locked myself in the bathroom so I could take a shower and hide in case Jyion came looking for me. I waited until I heard his car start before coming out of the bathroom and heading to the spare room. Opening the door, I could hear Nevaeh snoring as I grabbed a tee shirt and shorts out of the dresser and got in the king-sized bed to go to sleep. As soon as my head hit the pillow, my hair smelled like Jyion and I fell asleep replaying the sex we'd just had.

I could feel the sun on my face, and it felt like warm kisses. Kisses from my mother and father a long time ago. I loved the feeling. The breeze was caressing my face and I could feel the smile that had been missing for so long. I could smell the smell of my mother. She smelled like flowers, sweet and light. I could hear the sizzle of the oil as she fried me plantains and the clink clink of the spoon hitting the mug as she mixed us chocolate tea with the sweet milk.

"Treajure, wake up baby, or you ago late fi school," she would say.

I was calling out to her in my mind, but I couldn't wake up. Mama help I can't move. Then, I heard his voice. He was whispering so mama didn't hear him, "Trea, hurry up or I'm not waiting on you mi wan link up Sharon before class."

My brother Kaniel was always trying to sneak and mess around those nasty girls and they all loved him because he was so handsome. He was a pretty boy, with short, curly hair, dark brown skin that made him look exotic, dimples, and as if God didn't bless him enough, he had light grey eyes.

I could feel myself roll over because the sleep felt too good to wake up. I could feel Kaneil jumping on the bed and shaking me.

"KANEIL, stop it!" I jumped up and shouted.

Seeing Nevaeh sit up in the bed next to me, I realized I wasn't back in Jamaica. I was in New York at Sasha's house.

"I'm lost. Why are you dreaming about Sasha's baby's father?" she asked with a confused look on her face.

"Oh no Nev, it's nothing like that. Kaneil was my older brother. He was murdered before we moved here and it was my fault," I said the last part quietly because it's not something I really wanted to say out loud. I'd been thinking it for three years, but saying it out loud made it seem so real. I thought I couldn't cry over his death anymore, but I was sitting there with tears running down my face, dripping onto the pink blanket in front of me into a small puddle. I couldn't help but cry. I missed my brother. He was my hero, and when he was killed I felt like a piece of me was taken. Kaneil was two years older than me and it was just me, him, and our mom for as long as I could remember. Our father went to England when I was a kid and never came back. He would send us stuff sometimes and make sure my mom had enough money for us to eat, but nothing special. Feeling Nevaeh give me a side hug, I started to feel embarrassed. I hadn't cried over my brother in a long time.

"Treajure, maybe you should talk about what happened. We've been friends for a few years now, and you never talk about anything from before we met. Shit, I see how much you still love your baby's father, but you won't even tell him y'all got fucking kids. What did he do, kill your brother or something?"

Not even knowing where to start my story, I sat staring out of the window for a long time, watching the clouds pass over the sun. Thinking back to the day that started it all, the day I just dreamed of, shit it was so real.

"Nevaeh I will tell you the story, but I don't really think it will help me or that it's worth telling."

"That same morning I was dreaming about, after I got out of bed, I brushed my teeth and washed my face and I threw my uniform on. I remember poking my head out of my room to make sure my mother was gone to work. I had used some safety pins to make my skirt shorter and show off more of my legs. I spent like an hour in the mirror over my dresser taking the brush and trying everything I could to control the curls in my hair. It was May and already ninety-three degrees outside. The heat was making my hair frizz up. Finally giving up, I used a white head-band to at least keep it out of my face. As a final touch, I used some strawberry lip-gloss, making kissy faces at the mirror. Thinking I was cute, I finally decided to hurry up before my brother left me."

"I tried to casually ask my brother if Jyion was walking with us as we walked to school. Jyion was his best friend and he used to walk with us every day, but for whatever reason that day he wasn't there and I was missing his ass. He was so fine to me, and I loved being in his presence."

"That's why your little fast ass got on that short skirt and grown lip gloss on. Treajure you better not be looking at no boys, especially Jyion. I'mma kick your ass that's what's gonna happen," I mimicked my brother fussing at me.

"Honestly, I wasn't even listening. I was thinking about Jyion and how he walked so sexy with his bow legs, and how his voice sounded when he would call my name. There was something about him. He wasn't a pretty boy like my brother. He had skin the color of dark chocolate, dark colored eyes, and even then he had the scar on the side of his face that ran from behind his left ear to under his chin. When I was ten and he was thirteen, another boy cut him in a fight. I cried for days after that until I knew he was ok. Shit, I liked him even back then.

When She's Your Everything

"Finally that day we reached the school yard and it took all I had in me to not roll my eyes in Kaneil's face. I was almost sixteen and I felt I didn't need anyone telling me what to do or how to do it. Seeing him run off to hug the girl Sharon and grab her booty, I went to find Sasha, who was my best friend even back then. She started fucking wit' me too.

"'Trea, who are you looking cute for today girl, you know my cousin is not even here to notice you but I am sure someone will,' I remember her asking. She laughed, knowing how I felt about Jyion. As that day went on, I wished I wouldn't have worn the shorter skirt to school because boys were calling out to me and grabbing at my butt. I was so glad when the day was finally over. Standing outside waiting on Kaneil, he ran up to me all sweaty and out of breath. My brother was always sweaty. He used to play football, wait soccer I mean. I forgot that's what you guys call it. 'Treajure I have to stay late today, so gwan without me. Go straight home. No messing around and hanging out,' he told me before he turned around and ran up to some girl whose name I didn't even know.

"Shrugging my shoulders, I began the walk home by myself. I wasn't really worried; I mean, yea Jamaica could be dangerous for a young girl alone, but a lot of kids from my school were all walking the same way. Deciding to stop at the shop and get a juice and some banana chips, I took a small detour. I was so glad I did, because Jyion was sitting outside of the shop playing dominoes. As soon as I seen him, I felt shy all of the sudden. My hands were shaking and my palms where sweaty. I walked in the store, hoping him or no one else caught me staring. As I walked out, he was smiling and called out to me. he asked me where I was going and I told him I was on my way home from school. I waved and walked away with a little twist in my step, hoping he was looking at my ass.

"Walking down the alley that would take me home, I suddenly seen shadows behind me. As I turned around, what I saw made my heart drop. Four boys were following me with their faces covered in bandannas and knives in their hands. 'Hey girl, come here,' the biggest one called out to me. I was scared, but I tried to run anyway. It didn't do much good. They grabbed me and threw me to the ground."

"Oh my God Trea, were you raped?" Nevaeh interrupted my story.

"No. Jyion came in time to save me. He ran down the ally and stabbed two of the guys to death in front of me. I will never forget the smell of blood and the look on their lifeless faces. Their eyes were big with surprise. The other two boys ran away. That right there sealed my brother's fate, one of the same boys later murdered him as revenge. All because I was trying to be grown. All because I didn't listen to my brother."

"Damn Treajure, I'm sorry. You can't blame yourself, because no one should've been trying to rape you. So, if Jyion saved your life, why did you and him stop talking?" Nevaeh asked.

"Yea, I always wondered that. All of these years it made no sense to me," Sasha chimed in as she came in and threw herself on the bed. I guess she was listening in from the hallway. "Oh yea, and I heard you two nasty fuckers last night. Tell my cousin I want a new couch or carpet or whatever you two fucked on. I hope your ass not pregnant again," she laughed.

I laughed right along with her, trying to get the two of them to leave me alone about Jyion altogether and hoping that him busting in me one time didn't result in another pregnancy. Trying to get them to leave me along didn't work well, they were staring at me like the hyenas did little Simba in the Lion King.

"Look, I loved Jyion so much. After he saved me, he came to talk to me the next day about what happened and see if I was ok. I was in my bed crying, and no one else was home. I lied to my mom and told her I was not feeling well, so I stayed home from school. I was really just scared the two boys who got away were going to come and kill me because they threatened to kill us when they ran away. Jyion walked in and sat on my bed. Once he seen I was shaking, crying with snot coming out of my nose, I guess he felt bad. So he moved closer to me and held me in his arms. I will never forget what he said to me. He said, 'Treajure, I would die before I let someone hurt you. I love you.'

"Then he began kissing me and me and my fast ass was touching his dick and pulling it out of his pants. He took my virginity that day. I remember it hurt like hell. I never wanted to have sex again, but I felt like me and him had something from that moment on. He held me for a while after and told me a bunch of sweet nothings that really had me feeling special."

"I was a fool, young, and had been in love with him forever. I trusted him with my body and my heart, and he fucked that up. At first, he just started avoiding me. So I thought he just was afraid of my brother finding out that we had sex. After two months and me realizing I missed my periods added with the fact I couldn't keep down anything, I knew I was pregnant, but had no money to get a test so I tried to talk to him again."

Trying not to look at Sasha because I could see the sadness in her eyes, she knew what happened to the baby I was carrying. Well, she knew some of it.

"By the time I was four months, I was becoming frustrated because all Jyion would do is ignore me. I had to finally tell my mom and Kaneil I was pregnant, but I wouldn't tell them who the father was. I didn't want Kaneil and his best friend to have any problems because of me. I went and found a job as a mother's helper after school, and I would hand wash clothes and watch the little kids. I knew my mom couldn't afford another mouth to feed, so I was going to help myself since Jyion wouldn't.

"One day I was outside the school and was getting sick. I looked up, only to see this nigga Jyion leaning against a tree with his pants to his knees and this girl who I hated, Anita, sucking his dick. He just stared at me with his dark eyes blank, watching me throw up and struggle to catch my breath. I was so hurt. Before I slept with Jyion, we were friends. We always laughed and joked and hung out, but it was like he hated me for no reason after he had sex with me. I waited until early the next day and went to Sasha's house where he lived. His aunt, Miss Bell, let me right in and instead of going to Sasha's room, I went to his. He was laying in the bed with only his boxers on and a sheet covering him.

"I woke him up and he flipped out, started calling me names, and told me to stop lying on him saying I was pregnant. I was so angry I picked up the lamp and hit him right upside his fucking head. He grabbed me and threw me against the wall so hard the noise it made had the whole house running to see what happened. I was in so much pain but I was embarrassed, so I ran out the front door, not answering when anyone asked what happened. I ended up collapsing not far from the house. I was bleeding everywhere; I had lost our baby. He killed our baby.

"Thank God Covey was just coming in and found me. He took me to the hospital and made sure I was taken care of. I hated Jyion for breaking my heart. Then I hated him for killing our baby, even if he didn't mean it. But most of all, I hated him for not being there for me when I laid in that hospital bed, losing our son."

Looking at the girls, they were both crying. I'd never told anyone that full story out loud. I didn't really know what else to say. I guess I could tell them how we ended up with twins after all of that. I'm sure that is the next question from Sasha, I could see it in her eyes.

"I know you both want to know how we ended up with the twins, right?" I asked. Sniffling, Sasha and Nevaeh nodded their heads yes. "Kaneil was murdered five months after I lost the baby. By then

Sasha, you were pregnant and I was getting ready to come to Brooklyn. I went to Kaneil's grave before I left. I sat there and told him I was sorry, and I loved him. I know it seems stupid, but I needed to say goodbye to my brother. That's when Jyion showed up. Funny how all that time I tried to talk to him he ignored me, but when he was ready to say something he wouldn't stop trying. He tried to apologize and the apology turned into sex and that was the last time I seen him. I never would have thought I would have ended up pregnant again."

"I think you should tell him about the twins and forgive him. Carrying all of that hurt and anger can't be good for you," Nevaeh said, giving me another hug. Feeling drained from reliving that story, I rolled over and placed my face in the pillow to finish crying. Feeling Sasha rub my back, I drifted off to sleep wondering how I really felt about Jyion after all this time.

Chapter 4

Nevaeh

I was glad that the girls never asked me about the fight from the night before. I'm ashamed that I used to be friends with a bitch like Tauni. Thinking about the situation with her made me sad and angry at the same time and to think that she had the nerve to come for me after all of this shit. Also, I swore I saw her talking to Treajure's baby daddy. I just hoped that wasn't the case. If it was, Tauni is going to be a problem. I just knew it.

Wow. Sitting back and thinking about the whole situation with Jyion and Treasure, I wondered if I would ever have a deep love like the ones my home girls have experienced. Even though they both ended up with broken hearts, it was just circumstances that caused that. Shit, I think that they still have a chance at happily ever after. Even after hearing the story about Jyion, I still liked him better than that snake Lamar. There's just something about him. I always felt like I knew him from somewhere and couldn't put my finger on where. He seemed so soft to me. I think that's why Treajure has no respect for him. I guess I have love in my life. Me and my boyfriend Frank have been together for about four years, since high school, and he knows all about my situation growing up with no mom or dad. Both of my parents had me young, and just moved on with their lives when I was about two years old.

They both have new families and good jobs. My mom lives somewhere in L.A. and my dad is in Florida, last I heard. I think he married a white lady or some shit. It was hard not having parents growing up, and I think that makes me slightly insecure. These insecurities were probably one of the reasons I was still fucking with Frank. I mean I love him, but the love is just not the 'I will die if you leave me' kind of love.

I know I'm settling for Frank, because some days I wake up and feel like if my parents didn't want me, who is going to want me? Then I remind myself that Frank wants me and I know I have to settle for that. Walking from Sasha's house and hopping on the number ten bus that takes me towards Portland, I prepared to start my shift at work. I had an overnight shift tonight and a noon class tomorrow, so hopefully I won't have much paperwork to process and I can focus on some of this homework.

Taking out my Biology book, I began reading re-reading the same three sentences in the book. Instead of focusing on the actual words in front of me, all I could think about was Covey. He's not really my type; well I didn't think he was at least, since I've only been with one guy. Covey seemed so powerful and just yummy, yea I said yummy like a fucking bowl of ice cream or some skittles. I wondered if someone like him was capable of loving someone like me. I began to fantasize about him coming to take me away from Frank and making me his woman. I was imagining his lips on my bare skin when I heard the bus driver announce the stop for the hospital. Gathering my stuff, I walked off the bus and into the heat.

I process medical billing paperwork for Rochester General Hospital. It's an easy job and the money is good. God knows I need all the money I can get, because my portion of the tuition at the University of Rochester isn't cheap at all. I can only get basic financial aid, no loans or TAP, because I am under twenty-one, with no kids. They said they could use my parents' financial information, but since I had no real idea where my parents were that wasn't an option for me. There should be a waiver or something for people with special circumstances. Oh well, I didn't let that shit discourage me. I was going to be a research doctor and I planned to be the best in my field someday. I planned to find a cure for cancer. Cancer was what killed my aunt Dana. She was the person who raised me, showed me love, and I wouldn't let all the hard work she put into taking care of me be for nothing.

Finally making it to work, I tried to call my boyfriend Frank and see how he was, since he has been ignoring my calls all morning. He didn't even contact me last night to check on me. I was starting to get worried because that wasn't like him. Even when he was annoyed when I went out, most of the time he would talk shit in a text or something like that. Or try to find out what I was up to by asking dumb ass questions. After listening to the phone ring out like four times, he began sending me straight to voicemail. What the fuck was this nigga's problem. I kept getting a bad feeling in the pit of my stomach because I didn't know how he was ignoring me all of that time, now he's sending me to voicemail. Trying to stay positive, I gave him the benefit of the doubt. Someone must've stolen his phone, or maybe the battery was dead.

My shift was going fast tonight, and even though I'd been at work for six hours already, I still hadn't heard from Frank. I wanted to call his mom to see if he was ok, but since it was four AM I figured I should probably wait until a respectable hour. I decided to call him again, because I was starting to get annoyed. This time, his phone just rang and rang until it went to voicemail. I guess the fucking thing wasn't dead anymore, and still no phone call or response. I decided to send one last text and wash my hands of it. I would deal with this dickhead once I got home.

Me: *Frank what the fuck is going on? I was starting to get worried because I have been calling and texting you all day. I was even going to call your mother to make sure you were ok but I see your phone is no longer going to voicemail so I guess its fuck me and my feelings and you must be doing fine.*

Looking down at my fingernails, I felt sad. My nails are torn and tattered. I sometimes treated myself to a manicure and pedicure, and have them put gel paint on my fingers. But lately I haven't been able to. Frank had stopped giving me extra money for about the last six months. He still paid the bills at the apartment and made sure we had food to eat, but it seemed like he stopped caring about my personal needs. I just assumed there was no money for extras; I know when a man is in the streets, times get hard. So, I never questioned Frank because I didn't want to add to any stress. Now I was wondering if it was something else. Was he cheating on me? I didn't know when he came home every night whether he was out handling business or not, and I had never gotten any phone calls from bitches. I never saw any calling him, and yea I do check his phone and pockets on the regular.

Shit, no wonder Covey had jokes when he met me. My nails weren't done and I had on old tights and a plain neon green tank top with matching old navy flip flops. I was taking the bus to Treajure's house, so I didn't dress up that day. I had on no make-up, which I don't normally wear anyway, and my long hair was pulled into a messy bun. When I walked through the front door, I couldn't help but stare. He was delicious looking, like a bowl of ice cream on a hot summer night. Hearing my text alert go off interrupting dirty thoughts about me and my friend's brother, I hurried and looked at the screen. Finally, frank responded to me after all of this time.

Frank: *Look B stop texting and calling me, we are done. I have moved on and I don't want anything to do with you anymore. I suggest you get your shit as soon as possible you know this area it will be gone* *by the time the sun comes up and I don't want to see your face around here again.*

Me: *Frank stop playing, are you drunk or something? That is my home what you mean you don't want to see my face again. We been together for years and now you are what breaking up with me via text message? I know this shit can't be for real.*

Frank: *Bitch yea it's for fucking real. I heard all about the lies and shit you told my mom. About me hitting your dumb ass and how I am stealing from my job. I am done with you, this is the last straw. You are very fucking hard headed. I told you to quit school a long time ago and to get that stripping job to help a nigga out but no you wouldn't listen so now I don't need you and I am all set.*

Sitting there looking at the phone, I didn't really know what to say or do. I hurried and finished all the forms I had left on my desk before approaching my manager Natalie.

"Hey Natalie, I'm all done for the night. Can I leave a bit early? I have a class tomorrow and I could use the extra rest if you don't need me."

She looked at her desk, slowly checking the contents of the piles she had in front of her like she was trying her hardest to find me some more work to do. But seeing that I'd completed everything as I do every time I step in the building, she looked her pointy nose up and met my eyes.

"That is fine. Nevaeh. Have a nice day."

I almost ran out to the front door near the emergency exit so I could grab a taxi quick and get to my house. The whole way across town, I kept tapping my fingers on the door, wishing the driver would hurry up. I mean shit, it's five AM and no one was driving or on the roads, so I don't know why we had to go so fucking slow. As soon as we pulled up, I jumped out.

"Sir, I need you to please wait for me. I'm just going to grab a few of my things and I will be right back," I yelled running to the door.

I knew his ass wasn't moving because I didn't pay him yet. Taking the front steps two at a time, I was sweating and out of breath by the time I made it to the door. Putting my key in the lock, I noticed the key wouldn't fit.

"FRANK, open the fucking door, you bitch ass nigga," I began screaming and kicking the door, tears flowing down my face out of frustration and anger.

Looking at the driveway, I noticed that his red Lexus was missing, and that's when I saw all the bags and boxes of stuff. What the fuck? My brown teddy bear that Frank bought me when we were dating in high school was peeking out of the top of one of the garbage bags. Snatching it open, I noticed my panties and bras were also in that bag. Going from bag to bag, all of my stuff was there, out on the street, ready to be stolen and picked up by the nearest crack head. And in this neighborhood, that wouldn't have taken long.

Ripping the head off the teddy bear and leaving it at the door step, I gazed at the lifeless eyes on the tiny helpless face and felt the same. I began moving everything to the taxi, thanking God he was in a van and not a car. He was ok with me loading up once I offered extra money, but mister lazy ass didn't lift a finger to help. I could feel tears trapped behind my eyes. I didn't want to cry in front of this guy who I didn't know, even though I knew my face was already tearstained. I got in the back of the car, not knowing where to go next.

"Can you pull into the ally across the street? I need to wait and see something before I leave."

Seeing he was about to make a complaint, I pulled out two hundred dollar bills and threw them on the seat next to him. Money talks, and even though it hurt to spend anything knowing I have to pay my fall tuition soon and I had no idea what my next move was, I need to see what this pussy was up to. I was gonna find out if I had to sit out there all night. I could call Treajure or Sasha, but I didn't want to be an inconvenience to them, and I was embarrassed at how stupid I was for letting Frank play me and throw me out of the house I lived in.

After waiting two hours, I was ready to leave. The driver was on his phone playing some Candy Crush game, and I was ready to get in someone's bed and fall asleep. That's when I saw his car swoop in the driveway. After what seemed like forever, but was actually about five minutes, he slid his chubby ass out of the car and walked to the passenger door. *What the hell is he doing?*

Seeing him reach in and come up with a brown-skinned chick who was rocking a striped maxi dress and a big ass pregnant belly, I could feel my blood boil. Did this motherfucker move a bitch in to our home and kick me out? Naw, he ain't crazy to do no shit like that. But I guess he was, because the next thing he was doing was taking out suitcases from the trunk. Miss Pregnant was standing there hugging him and smiling like they had pulled up at the Ritz instead of some run-down apartment building in Ghost Town.

I was in shock but the rage I was feeling got my feet moving fast. I snatched open the door so fast the driver's head shot up and his neck made a cracking noise.

"Really Frank? You think you can put me out of my house for another bitch? A side bitch?" I shouted as I ran at the two of them, ready to tear this girl's ass up for ruining my life.

"Who are you? And I know you're not calling me a bitch. My man and me are moving in together so our kids can have a two-parent household. My son misses his daddy when he's not home, and now that we have another one on the way…well you know. Or maybe you don't since I don't know who your man is," she said, while rubbing her belly and smirking at me.

Did this bitch just say son? As in a previous child? Oh hell no! Picking up the closest suitcase, I began swinging at both of them. I caught her in the back as she tried to run, and her crying out in pain and rolling on the ground made my heart sing. Feeling Frank grab me, I was only able to hit his legs a few times. Biting his nearest arm as hard as I could, I knew that it hurt because I felt him tense up and release his grip.

"Fuck you, stupid bitch. What is wrong with you?" He screamed.

"Frank, you're what's wrong with me. Your lies and games and the way I wasted four years of my fucking life with a man who has baby mommas and shit. So you're what's wrong with me, and Frank when you miss me or need me don't fucking call." Kicking him in his fat ass stomach one good time, I spit in his face, held my head up high and walked back to the taxi.

Feeling crushed, I leaned my head back on the sticky seat and sighed. Realizing I had to make a choice on where to go, I pulled out my phone to call Sasha. As soon as I clicked on her name I got some message saying my service was not active. So this nigga was playing a lot of games. He had my phone turned off. This shit was so petty when he was clearly the one in the wrong. The one who had been cheating on me all of this fucking time. Deciding to go to a hotel and then get my phone taken care of later, I told the driver to take me to the Holiday Inn near the airport. I hoped it wasn't too expensive. I didn't pick the Double Tree because I knew that one would be way out of my spending zone, and since my phone was down I didn't have time to be comparing rates and shit.

As soon as we pulled up to the hotel, I grabbed a bell boy and a cart, and loaded all of my stuff on it. Checking in, I was informed it would be one nineteen a night, so I booked three days and made my way to room number 301. I didn't bother to unpack anything or hang anything in the closet since I wouldn't be staying long. I had a little in my bank account, but once I paid my tuition and purchased books for the fall semester, there wouold be no way I could afford a hundred dollars a night on a place to stay. Calling T-mobile prepaid on the room phone, I made a payment on the phone and had it switched to my name only, so Frank no longer had access to my account. Taking a blazing hot shower, I got in the bed, hugging a pillow, and crying myself to sleep.

After sitting in the hotel for two days crying and wondering exactly where I went wrong with me and Frank, I decided it was time to get up and make a plan. I only had one full day left at the hotel and had a room full of stuff with nowhere to go. I went through all the boxes, bags and suitcases, and decided to repack and get rid of stuff that was no longer worth me keeping. When I was finished, I had twelve suitcases, four boxes and seven garbage bags filled with stuff. Calling U-haul storage, I got the smallest storage space available for only sixty dollars a month. Then I called the five-dollar cab and offered him twenty to take me three places. one was school, so I could put as many clothes as I could in two lockers I'd claimed and put locks on. The second was to my job, so I could lock up the important stuff in my desk, and pick up my paycheck. The last was the storage place.

Keeping a duffel bag with five outfits, one pair of shoes, and my personal items in it, along with my book bag for school, I was all set to go… well, I didn't know where I was going after the next morning when I had to check-out of the hotel. University of Rochester took their payment of six thousand and fifty-eight dollars, and my checking account was almost at zero. Deciding to splurge on some Country Sweet Chicken, kind of like a last meal, I stopped there before heading back to the Holiday Inn.

*****

The next morning, I called Treajure and she didn't answer. When I called Sasha she was going off about something Ajay did, so I kept my problems to myself. Packing up the little bit of stuff I had, I headed out the door walking towards Walmart so I could hop on a bus to somewhere near school, I guess. Deciding to kill time, I went to McDonald's and got lunch, slowly picking over my food so I had some place to sit and charge my phone. I was there almost three hours before the manager asked me to leave.

Getting on the bus, I headed to my old apartment building on Monroe Ave. The Strathmore is where me and my Aunt Donna used to live. I knew that no one used the back door much, especially at night, so it would be a good place to rest up until tomorrow. On the walk from the bus stop to the apartment, all I could think about is how great my life used to be and I took it for granted. Maybe I could have been better to Frank. I could've listened to his suggestions, or fucked him more. Even gave him a baby. Who would have thought all those days I laid in my queen-sized bed, watched TV until I fell asleep, and dreamed about living the "life," that I was already living the life.

Waiting until I saw someone with a key open the door and come inside, I came in behind them acting like I lived there.

"Thank you," I said, smiling at the old grey haired lady as she held the door for me and my heavy bags. Heading to the elevator, I waited until she got off on the fourth floor, and made my way back to the first. Heading past the apartments on the left, I found the door I was looking for and pushed it open. There was a little entry way with black and white checkered tile on the floor, and another heavy glass door that led to outside. Sinking to the floor, I used the nearby brick as a pillow as I clutched my bags close and fell asleep.

Chapter 5

Jyion

Pulling out of Sasha's , drove home in no real rush. I knew once I got there, I would have to deal with Tauni's annoying ass and I didn't want to put hands on her since she's pregnant wit' my seed. I was still shocked at seeing Treajure and feeling Treajure. I missed that girl like fucking crazy all of these years. I'd been looking for her since I'd been in the town. Even before then, but I assumed she was still in Brooklyn with her aunt because I had yet to catch up with her. Then yesterday, Aunt Fi tells me that Treajure's been living here since her twins were almost a year old and she goes to college and is doing good for herself.

I was stuck when I heard that shit. I mean, yea I heard she had a kid, but twins? And where the fuck was their punk ass daddy at, because I'd been giving money to Covey to help take care of Trea all this time. She'll always be my first baby moms, so I am gonna always check for her. I didn't think any other nigga was taking care of her and the kids, or Covey would have told me to stop sending her bread. Even though I wouldn't have. Hell, if this nigga would've told me another man was in the picture, I would have lost it. I can't picture Treajure with anyone but me. She still thinks Covey is the one giving her money and making sure she's all set. I never wanted her to know I was involved because I knew how much she hated me and I knew her stubborn ass wouldn't have accepted anything from me had she known. Shit, she's so hardheaded, her and the twins would probably be living in the streets.

As soon as I pulled into the driveway of my house in Henrietta, I could see all the downstairs lights on. Here we go with the nonsense as soon as I step in. I should've stayed at Sasha's and cuddled with Treajure. She's going to have to stop running from me because we're going to be together. I just have to get rid of Lamar and whoever her baby daddy is, and we're good to go. Oh yea, and I have to handle my situation as well. I don't know what I was thinking getting involved with this girl and now she's pregnant. I guess I forgot the hardest part in my plan, getting Trea to forgive me, to fall back in love with me. After tonight, I don't know if that's as impossible as I used to think it was. Thinking about her tight, wet pussy had my dick hard as fuck again. I hope I got her pregnant, that's why I nutted in her ass on purpose.

Tina Marie

The front door creaked open when I walked in. Tauni popped up from the couch like a fucking jack in the box, her braids swinging so hard one hit her in the eye and she had to stop for a whole minute until it stopped watering.

"For real Jyion, you're just coming home? You couldn't check on me and you snatched another bitch, a bitch who stabbed my best friend, and left with her? You're a loser and I am sorry I'm stuck having a baby with your careless ass."

She began crying hysterically and sounding like a hyena. Then she threw the clear glass vase next to the couch at my fucking head. Moving to the side as the vase hit the wall and the pieces shattered to the floor, I rushed over to her and snatched her by those fucking hideous braids she had.

"Bitch, I'm a fucking man, so don't question me, I knew you was aight the way you kept calling and FaceTimeing my fucking phone all night long. I took my family home after some shit popped off. I didn't even know you were there since I told your ass to stay the fuck home. You don't know how to act in a club, or anywhere for that matter, and I don't want my baby harmed."

Looking at her, I knew she was going to forever be a pain in my ass. She's gorgeous. Her light skin is flawless with high cheekbones and long eyelashes that framed her light brown eyes, but her attitude is ugly. Right now, her nose is bright red and her eyes are filled with tears, but I don't feel sorry for her or anything I did. If she would've stayed the fuck home, this wouldn't be a problem.

When She's Your Everything

I met Tauni at a bar one night and she was dressed in some jeans and a little ass shirt with her belly out. She was adorable and seemed like she carried herself well. It was winter and she wasn't naked like most of the other girls, and even though her friends were pissy drunk, she seemed to not even be drinking. She bought me a drink and had the bartender send it to me. I thought it was a cute way to flirt with me, so I hollered at her.

She let me fuck her on the first day in the alley outside of the bar. That should've been a huge warning sign, but I was still trying to fuck wit' her. Shit, she had some good pussy and swallowed my dick like a pro. The first time I went to her house to chill, I was cool with it because her shit was clean. I mean, she ain't have much furniture but there was a couch and a TV and shit.

I was thrown off when I noticed a folding chair in front of her front window and one section of blinds that looked like a rat ate them. It took me a few visits to realize that this bitch sat at the window all day, watching her neighbors and shit. Getting her pregnant was not a part of my plan, but it seemed like it was a part of hers, because she was way too happy when she came and brought me the news. Now she was like a thorn in my side, one I couldn't get rid of. I only have her staying in my crib because she's way more reckless than she appeared at first, and I want to make sure my seed is cool. She's nosey; loves to drink, party and, you guessed it, fight. The list goes on and on.

Yanking my jeans and boxers down with one hand I snatched her head and pulled it towards my rock hard dick. Not giving her annoying ass a chance to say a word, I shut her up the only way I knew how, by fucking her mouth with no remorse. All I could think about was Treajure's pretty breasts that were looking perfect in that white shit she had on. Damn, she was so soft and smelled good, like some perfume and baby powder mixed together. Seeing Tauni choke, I eased out a bit.

"Yo, open your mouth and catch this shit, girl." I began jerking my shit off with the tip of my dick on her tongue. I came so hard it was all over her face and breasts, even dripping on my carpet. Seeing her lick it up, I just kept going because that was turning me on. Knowing I didn't want to fuck her tonight, I pushed myself deeper in her mouth until I finally felt myself go limp.

"Clean this up and bring your ass to bed. Don't be breaking shit else in my crib, or you gonna have to move on out, baby or no baby. I don't do all that reckless shit," I said as I went to shower. Damn, she was sucking all of Treajure's pussy juice off my shit. I never even wiped my dick off when I left Sasha's place. Oops.

I guess the dick shut her ass up for real because she was lying in the bed with her back to the bathroom door, lightly snoring. Grabbing the remote, I turned the TV on to some movie on HBO and tried to fall asleep. All I kept thinking about was seeing Treajure after all this time. She was the girl I really loved, but we had too much against us. I was friends with her big brother, and he made it clear he didn't want me and her to hook up. I never made my feelings known to her. After she was attacked and she saw me kill someone, I felt like I needed to be near her, and then *bam*. I fucked around and took her virginity.

I always felt like the attack was my fault. Well, mine and Kaneil's. One of the boys I killed was this cat named Jason. He was a young dude who used to hustle his little drugs in the tourist area to all the Americans looking to get high while they were on the island. And it was a good hustle. A week before the attack, me and Kaneil decided to cut school and rob Jason. Being young and stupid, we didn't make an effort to hide our identity. I remembered feeling like I was the man back then, when I was really just a dumb ass lil' nigga. Shit, things were tough back then. I mean they still are now, but at least as an adult we have the upperhand in this drug business. As kids, we lived dirt poor. That money was the start to our come up and nothing was going to stop us from our plan.

I really fucked up where Treajure is concerned. Once I pulled her in for that brief moment, she fell in love with me for real, no more baby crush. But I was too young to be tied down and I had to make sure to show her I was not the kind of nigga she needed in her life. All I could see was killing, robbing, and stacking bread in my future, and I knew it would be dangerous for her. So I fucked with a bunch of bitches, and made sure she saw when I did. I wanted to hurt her but I didn't want to, you know. I figured if I hurt her she would stay away from me, and then I didn't have to worry about her being harmed again, or worse, because of me and my actions. I didn't want to hurt her because I loved her. I mean, my whole life she was always there, as an annoying little kid to a cute pre-teen to a bad ass teenager with hips and breasts looking like whoa. She had other qualities, too. She always made me smile and laugh when we were around each other, and she was smart as hell. I noticed all of this stuff long before I slept with her. But once I was inside of her brand new pussy, I knew I couldn't leave her alone. But that I had to.

When I noticed her belly getting big and how she was throwing up everywhere she went, I knew she was pregnant and that it was mine. The day I was getting topped off by the school and she was there getting sick, it took everything in me to ignore her. I thought she was going to die, that's how sick she looked. But my life, back then, was out of control. See, we didn't just rob Jason. We robbed a few other people after that, and it was catching up to us. Just that week I was shot at in a neighboring parish after a lick, and word on the streets was that Jason's family wanted revenge for his death. It was more dangerous for her to be with me until I could handle all of my enemies. When she came to see me and I slammed her up against the wall, I knew she was pregnant. I knew and I still shoved her hard, and watched her get up in pain and walk away, bleeding. Honestly, it was a reaction. I mean fuck, she hit me first. I ran out after her, but it was too late. Covey had already left in a taxi to take her to the hospital, and her love for me had turned to hate.

Taking out my phone, I texted Sasha, asking her to give me Treajure's number. She read the text even though it's like five in the morning, but never responded. I guess her little ass forgot she got her fucking read message on her IPhone. Texting her that I'mma kick her ass, I rolled over and tried to get some sleep. Waking up early, I smelled something cooking in the kitchen. But since Tauni's ass was making it, I was all set on that. Her food looked like something a pig shit out. Picking up the phone to see if Sasha text me back, I saw she sent me the middle finger and a laughing emoji, and that's all. Aight, they want to fucking play wit' me, I got something for their slick asses, thinking I won't get to my girl. After handling my hygiene, I got up and called Tavian to see what the fuck he was up to.

"Son, what's up?" I asked as he answered on the second ring.

"Shit, not a thing. I am just here in the crib eating some food and texting this chick on the phone," he responded with an odd tone in his voice.

"Since when you text bitches on the phone? Or anyone? That's not even your style. Anyway, I am about to go to Sasha house and snatch Treajure's little ass up. I dropped her off there last night and I realized I can't let her go again, not this time. I mean, all that shit in the past I'm trynna make it right. But she's fighting me on it. Anyway, we need to get up and talk about this new shipment later, so just hit me up when you ready."

Sitting on the phone talking shit to my nigga, I started throwing on some clothes. Nothing fancy, just some Adidas soccer shorts and a wife beater wit' some Adidas slides. Throwing my chain on and making sure I tucked my gun in my waist, I looked in the mirror one last time. That's when I caught a glimpse in the hallway. That bitch Tauni was there listening to my conversation, probably the whole time.

Smirking at her as I made my way out the door, I hopped in my all-white Range Rover and made my way to Sasha's house. Not bothering to knock, I used the key and walked in.

"What the fuck, Jy? You don't live here. I'm tired of you and fucking Covey just rolling up in my crib like y'all own the place," Sasha whined as I moved around her and headed up the stairs.

"Hey Sasha, what you gonna do about it?" I laughed and began checking rooms, looking for Treajure. I knew her ass still in here somewhere. The second room I checked, yup, shawty was in there, Treajure was laid out on her back with only a tiny ass shirt and some panties on. Hearing Sasha run up the stairs, I hurried and stepped in, closing and locking the door. I hoped she didn't start beating on it or no wild shit, she goes hard for her bestie.

Waiting a few minutes and not hearing anything, I began taking my clothes off so all I had on was my boxers. I placed my two phones and my gun on the dresser and eased myself on the bed slowly, so I wouldn't wake her up. I rolled on my side and pulled her close to me. I just wanted some time with her in my arms, in my presence. Letting my eyes roam her almost naked body, I couldn't believe how great she looked after having twins. Her body was still firm and slim in all the right places; no other girl could compare to her even a little bit.

Leaning near her face, I whispered in her ear, "I miss you Treajure."

She snuggled closer to me, rubbing her breasts against my bare chest. Running my tongue along the curve of her neck and making my way down her body, I lifted her shirt and kissed her navel, taking time to play with the colorful belly ring that she had in, before making my way further down. As soon as my mouth got to her fat pussy, my kissing her through that little ass thong made her jump up.

"Jyion, what the hell are you doing here? Get out," she shrieked, pushing me off of her. Too bad for her frail arms that I'm way stronger than she was. Dipping my head to kiss her lips, I got lost in that kiss. I moved her little piece of panties to the side and slid in her warmth. Feeling her move her body to my rhythm, I began to go deeper. Breaking the kiss, she took in a deep breath and I put her legs on my shoulders. She began shaking and moaning.

"Yes, Treajure. Cum for me, baby. I want to feel that pussy quint on my dick."

Grabbing her and turning her over, I almost had a heart attack when I worked my way in and she started winding her pussy.

"Throw it back girl, just like that."

Watching her ass bounce, I knew I couldn't hold back much longer. Grabbing her and taking over, I began moving faster. It was like my dick had a mind of its own, and as soon as she came again, I was right behind her. I came so strong, it made my belly cramp.

"Jyion, pull out," she mumbled, but it was too late for that. I bet her ass ain't on no birth control, either.

"Hush girl, you good. Go back to sleep," I responded, laughing. Surprisingly, she did just that and went back to sleep in my arms.

Her phone was getting on my nerves. Every five minutes, it was buzzing on the nightstand next to us. Fuck it, I'm the kind of dude that doesn't give a fuck, so I'mma just answer it.

"Yo?" Hearing some whiney ass nigga on the other end, I almost laughed. But I'mma save the laughter until he asks where Trea at.

"Man, who the fuck is this answering my woman's phone?" he kept crying into the line. Now I was laughing, I couldn't even help myself. Treajure snatched the phone out my hand and ran in the bathroom to go soothe her bitch ass nigga's feelings.

"Yo Trea, I'm gone for now. I'm gonna holla at you later," I yelled through the door, still laughing.

Chapter 6

Sasha

Opening the door to my house while holding Kaneil Jr. in one arm and a bag of groceries in the other, I almost tripped over a pair of Timberland boots as soon as I walked in. Urghhh, this motherfucker is so lazy, and this is why we can't live together. I don't like people in my space. Who in their right mind would leave a big ass pair of boots in the doorway of the front door? See, it's stuff like this that makes me not want to fuck with Ajay's ass and I'm surely regretting giving his whining ass a key. Ever since my brother has been around, Ajay started acting real insecure and saying that I'm going to leave him because my brother and cousin are in town. So, I gave him a key to show him that our relationship was moving forward. Setting down the bags of groceries on the counter, I picked the big black boots up and threw them down the basement stairs.

"Sasha, what is that noise? I know you not throwing my fucking shoes," he bitched from upstairs. Lucky for him, my ignore game is tight. Feeling how heavy my baby is in his sleep, I decided to hurry and put him in his bed.

As soon as I laid him down and made it to my room, I smelled something in the air that was not just weed. I know mister dummy is not smoking anything in my house. It smelled like weed mixed with a sour aroma, and topped off by the air freshener that is not doing any good to cover it. Sniffing the air some more, I swear I smelled pussy in here. I hope, no I pray for his sake, that he did not fuck a girl in my house.

"So Ajay, what did you do all day? And what are you smoking?" I questioned as I stood over him with my arms folded, while he's lying in my bed with a smile on his face. I can't believe he's looking so calm and I'm raging inside. If it wasn't for the fact that my son was home, I would've been punching him in his head already.

"Sasha, I'm not a kid, so don't question me. I don't have to tell you shit about what I was doing. I'm a grown ass man and you're not my mama," he said as he jumped up and shoved past me.

At the last minute, I pushed my foot in his path and his ass tripped and flew out into the hallway. Hearing a thud, I braced myself for some kind of comeback from this nigga. But after a few minutes, I didn't see his face. So, I calmly sat down on the bed and began taking my shoes off. I was tired from a long day working in my cousin's hair shop. Hearing him storm down the stairs mumbling, "stupid bitch," and hearing the downstairs door slam, I guess he wasn't going to fuck with me after I tripped his ass.

Lifting up the sheets and smelling and looking to see if everything looked the same as when I left, I still stripped the bed even though it all still seemed fresh. I wasn't taking any chances. Throwing away the turquois blue sheets, I went to the linen closet and got out the white and orange ones. These sheets were so cute with the little orange princess crowns printed on them. I'm sad because the blue ones where my favorite. They felt like silk, but I'm not taking a chance with this nasty nigga. Grabbing my white, bright green and orange striped comforter, I began the process of changing the bed. I love bright colors and my room was full of bright turquois blue, lime green, orange, and pink. My headboard was white leather and my curtains were white with pink panels in the middle. Man, I really love my room; I have all-white faux fur throw rugs, a pink accent wall behind my bed, and an all-white lounge chaise on the wall near my windows. That's my favorite spot to hang out and read, or just relax.

As soon as I finished making the bed, I was so tired I sat there naked and zoned out for a few minutes. My phone ringing brought me out of it. Answering it, but not looking at it first, I didn't realize it was a FaceTime call. Trying to cover my breasts with my hand once I did, I heard Tavian laughing as his face popped on the screen. I jumped in my bathrobe fast, before he really got a good look.

"Hey, what's good ma?" his deep voice came across the line. Seeing his face made me smile. He was outside somewhere, leaning up against a black truck, looking sexy as hell.

"Hey Tavian, I wasn't expecting you to call me. I'm not up to much, just got home from work and about to shower before my son wakes up. What you up to?" I asked as I sat on the bench to my vanity, holding the phone in front of me.

"Why would I take your number and not call you? Sasha you playing games, man. I'm not the bitch ass nigga you be fucking wit'. I am a real nigga, and I don't play around. So, when I'mma see you?"

"I don't know. When you have time, I guess," I responded, not knowing how I was going to get away with spending time with Tavian and having Ajay around.

I was really regretting giving him a key to my place more and more, because his ass is clingy and popped up all times of the day and night. He was always demanding to know where I was and what I was doing.

"Sasha, you still there, ma? I said I was out of town right now, but I will be in early tomorrow. So just meet me at IHOP for breakfast," Tavian told me, not asked me. I think that boss shit turns me on because I swear I was getting wet.

"Tavian, I will have my son tomorrow. I don't work on Mondays, and my aunt has him a lot when I work, so I don't know. Maybe I can get Neveah or Treajure to watch him so we can hang out. I can let you know in the morning," I said in an unsure tone. I kept thinking of all the reasons I wanted to see Tavian, and all the reasons I would have a hard time getting away.

"Yo Sasha, bring your son wit' you, and don't make me come to your house and pick you up. I don't give a fuck about who you live with, either. Meet me at ten tomorrow morning at the one in Greece."

Listening to the dial tone, I was just looking at the cell phone screen, trying to figure out if this rude fucker just told me what to do and hung up on me. I couldn't help but crack a smile. Trying to get away from Ajay was going to be interesting since he knows I am off on Mondays, and he likes for me to cook him breakfast on that day and spend time with him. Lying back on the bed, I started feeling depressed. I did hair a few days a week and my brother pays all my bills. I feel worthless. I didn't have a future with Ajay because he's just not the one and I didn't have a degree or anything for me to map out a future for myself. I was in school when I first got here, but I didn't stay focused. All I could think about was Kaneil and how I would never see him again, and how our son would grow up with no father. So, I ended up dropping my classes one semester and decided to go back, only I never did.

Picking up my IPad, I decided to look up what classes were open in the summer session so I could get back on track with my life. KJ was depending on me, and I couldn't let him down. Seeing Treajure call me and send me a message, I hit ignore and kept looking through the different days and times I could take some of the courses I needed. I felt bad that I'd barely talked to Trea and Nevaeh lately, but since Ajay comes in when he wants now and he doesn't like me talking on the phone to friends, or as he calls it gossiping, I just talk on the phone less. I didn't have the energy to argue with his ass every day. Speak of the devil, I heard his key turn in the lock downstairs. *Sigh, every time he comes in it makes me want to leave.*

Jumping on the bed and looking over my shoulder at my screen, his face turned into a frown.

"Sasha, what are you looking at? I know you are not looking at no school shit. That's not for you, ma. You good doing what you doing. If you want more money, my home boy got a strip club. Remember, the one I told you about? It's called Bikini Blazes and you really need to consider working there, because my man said he gonna give me a cut of the money if you come through. This shit will benefit both of us, babe."

"Naw, Ajay. I am not stripping or selling my body just to benefit you or anyone else. I am going back to school. I have a lot of credits. If I take summer classes, I will be able to catch up and get back into my business program, so I can open my exclusive salon/spa," I responded with a big ass attitude. I swear I understand how women become abusers of men, because some of these dudes act like their mommas put a pillow over they face or dropped them down several flights of stairs as babies. "Ajay, did your mom put rum in your baby bottle or what? You say the dumbest shit. I really can't get over this."

"Get over what you want to b, but you not going to no fucking school. It's a waste of time, and if you ain't stripping like I want, you need to be your ass up in this house wit' yo nigga," he said wit' some bass in his voice. Trying not to cry from frustration at this situation I'd gotten myself into, I just rolled over and waited for the morning to come. At least tomorrow I get to see Tavian.

"MOMMY," screamed my son, scaring me out of a deep sleep. Looking at the time on the cable box, I realized it was seven AM already, and I felt like I just went to bed. "MAMA COME, HELP ME," KJ screamed out again. I looked over at the still sleeping Ajay and hopped up to go see what was wrong with my baby.

Walking in, what I saw made my heart drop to my feet. On my son's robot sheets and all over his tangled up matching blue and white quilt were three grey mice. One was crawling on him and I noticed scratches and bites all over his legs. I hurried and snatched my baby off the bed, holding him close to me. I opened the closet to hurry and find him some clothes so we could get the hell out of this house. Seeing a set of my white sheets in his closet in a ball, I snatched them up trying to figure out what the fuck was going on. Throwing the sheets in the hallway and grabbing my baby some clothes, I hurried and slammed the door shut. Noticing a piece of paper fly out of the sheets I picked it up to look at later.

Taking all the stuff in the bathroom with me, I couldn't believe how KJ was shaking and crying from the pain and I didn't know what to do. Should I bathe him or call an ambulance? Throwing a blanket around him and shoving his clothes in my purse I ran to my room to grab my phone and throw on some sweats. Realizing I was still holding that note in my hand, I unfolded it and began to read: *Smell the sheets and know I was here fucking on your bed and if you don't believe that I hope my friends enjoyed your baby as a midnight snack. Sincerely, his true love.*

Oh *HELL* naw. This nigga done let some bitch come up in here and hurt my fucking baby. I am over this shit. Picking up the closest thing I could find at the moment, which was a broom, I smacked him right across his face. Jumping up out of his sleep, his dreads swinging in the air, he started yelling.

"Bitch, what the fuck is wrong with you? Do I hit yo' stupid ass? No, but you always got yo' hands on me."

Grabbing my bags and my baby, I threw the note and sheets in his face. "Get the fuck out of my house Ajay," I yelled, running down the stairs.

As soon as I made it to Park Ridge, they got my baby in a bed right away. He had an IV hooked up to him with medicine dripping into it and his legs where wrapped in bandages from the bites and scratches. Sobbing and holding KJ's hand, I didn't know what to do or who to call. My brother and cousin were going to kill Ajay, and probably me, if I told them what happened. Feeling my phone vibrate, I answered it.

"Hello," I could barely get out.

"Sasha you're not at the IHOP. What the fuck? I told you I wasn't playing games ma, and why you sound like that? You crying? I hope that fuck nigga didn't put his hands on you or nothing," Tavian blared into the phone. I totally forgot about him and breakfast. When it comes to my son, he had to come first.

"Tavian, I'm sorry but I cannot hang out with you today. I'm at Park Ridge with KJ, some crazy shit went down, and he got hurt. I'll make it up to you when I can," I explained.

"I am on my way," he said and hung up in my ear. *Damn, I hope Ajay took my advice and got the fuck out of my house, because what happens from here is out of my hands.* Kissing my baby on the head, I sat back in the chair and waited for the doctor to come in.

In less than ten minutes, the door flew open and Tavian was standing there in a pair of dark blue jean shorts, a black True Religion t-shirt, and some black sneakers. Today he only had on his earrings and watch, and his eyes had a more intense look. He leaned over the hospital bed and gently ran his hand over KJ's face.

"Is he ok? And why the fuck he got those bandages on?" he questioned, sitting down next to me in the blue plastic hospital chair. I gave him a sugar-coated explanation of what happened not wanting to be in the middle of a huge confrontation with him and Ajay.

"I woke up this morning to my son crying out and screaming because there were a few mice in his bed and they had bit and scratched his legs and his arm. So, I snatched him up, closed the bedroom door, and ran him here."

"Yo, were the mice came from? You living in the hood or some shit?" he questioned me.

"Tavian, I have never had a mouse or anything before. I don't know if it came from a neighbor or what. I'm going to put in a call to the landlord to have them come and take care of this shit, or I'mma move."

I felt bad lying about where the mice came from, but I have to do what I have to do. Seeing a bunch of texts come through, I opened up Ajay's.

Ajay: *Babe look I took care of the mice and even went and got little man a new comforter set and sheets. Yes, I washed them first. I can explain about what happened. I promise babes it's not my fault. I can't lose you and you know it. I will wait until you come home to talk. Love you girl.*

I had no words. He thinks it's that easy. That he can just do what he wants and there are no consequences? This is why I shouldn't have given him a key, because now I am going to have to struggle to get him out of my crib. Leaning over the railing of the bed, I grabbed KJ's hand and let the tears fall. I was crying for both of us, because now we're stuck in this horrible situation. Feeling Tavian pull me close to him, I let my tears soak his chest and I felt myself relax for the first time in a long time in the safety of his arms.

Chapter 7

Treajure

I haven't spent any quality time with Lamar in a few weeks. Since the incident with Covey, and then me having to explain all the bullshit with Jyion to him over the phone, things have been hectic. I mean Lamar is a good dude. He owns his own little business, a sneaker store called "The Spot," and he's usually respectful when dealing with me. I think he's been getting fed up with me because he wants something more serious than I do. Lamar is sexy; he stands five-foot-ten and has creamy brown skin like the caramel candies from the Werther's commercials. His waves are always on point, and he dresses ok, wears too many sneakers, but I be dressing him the way I want, so that's not a huge problem. He even has a handful of brown freckles across his cheeks that make his face pop.

Tina Marie

Feeling guilty, I decided to invite Lamar on a date. I mean, I was just busting it open for my baby daddy twice in a row, and I need to get him all the way out of my life and get shit together wit' the man I have, so I need to start somewhere. Pulling on some cheetah print tights and a black crop top, I ran the brush through my hair one time, threw on some black flip flops and I was ready. Looking in the mirror by the front door, I blew myself a lip gloss kiss and skipped out. I jumped in my car because I still didn't want Lamar at my house, so I told him I would meet him at the movies.

"Hey babe," I said as I saw him waiting for me outside the doors. I gave him a hug and he kissed me on the cheek. It felt so fake. I felt like I should've been patting him on his back like I would a stranger that I'm hugging. There's no heat or sizzle when we touch. I think I'm expecting too much from him. I need to just be happy that I have a good man who wants to be with me.

"Hey Treajure, you look nice today," he responded as he opened the door for me to enter the theater.

After we decided to watch the new Ghostbusters, I made my way to the concession stand to get some popcorn and nachos.

"Can I have a medium popcorn with extra butter, an order of nachos, a slushie and a pack of sour candies?" I placed my order and stepped aside so Lamar could pay.

"Trea, you do not need all of that shit to eat. We're going to dinner after and you're getting a little round lately, so you don't need all of this junk. As a matter of fact, I'm not paying for you to get fat,"

Lamar threw at me as he walked away from the counter, leaving me in front of the cashier looking played. Beyond mad, I opened my purse and pulled out some money to pay for my own stuff. So this nigga wanted to try and play me? Ok cool, because now I'm pissed, and after this movie, I am going the fuck home and not to any dinner with his ass. Two can play at that game.

The whole movie, I sat and ate my snacks and played with my phone. I wasn't even texting anyone, I was playing some word game that buzzed every time you got an answer wrong. So it seemed like someone was texting me. I was getting answers wrong just to get the phone to buzz more and piss him off; by the way his body was sitting in the chair all stiff, I could tell it was working. How dare his cheap ass not pay for my snacks. I mean, I got it trust me, but fuck him. My mind began to wander to the way Jyion was fucking me the other day, and I had to wiggle around in my chair to calm myself down. Jyion hadn't called me since he came and fucked me again, and I felt sad on one hand but relieved on the other. I needed him to stay away from me because him coming around complicated my life way too much.

As soon as the movie ended and we walked out, Lamar tried snaking his arm around my shoulders, but I brushed him off. I know he don't think everything was all good. Speed walking to my car, I turned to see him following behind like a little puppy.

"Lamar, since my ass is fat, I don't require dinner. So, I am going to be on my way," I threw at him as I opened the door and hopped in my Maxima. Looking out the window, I saw him standing there talking. But I guess he was about to be talking to his damn self, since I peeled out of the parking spot, almost running his feet over.

Turning up *Big Bumper* by Tifa, I began dancing in my leather seats and singing. If Lamar doesn't like my big ass, then someone else will. He better straighten up and fast, or I'm done with him. Since my plans were cancelled, I guess I would grab a bottle of wine and some take out from my favorite place, Olive Garden. Once I got my stuff for a Netflix and chill alone night, I made my way home.

I put Lamar on the block list since he refuses to stop calling my phone, and I am not in the mood. Setting my stuff on the glass table in my living room, I noticed the stack of the money Covey gave me to buy the kids' summer stuff was still sitting there. I'm going to get my babies tomorrow and take them to do some shopping and go to Chuckie Cheese; I almost forgot all about the money laying there.

I didn't even make it through one movie before I fell asleep on the couch. Waking up early, I felt like showing out today, so I put on some tight jean capris with rips up the front and a cut up white shirt that showed my tattoo of a diamond on my back and had my stomach out, showing off my pink heart belly ring. Slipping my feet into some all-white Adidas sneakers and putting on my silver bangles and silver hoop earrings, I was ready to touch the road. Spraying myself with Burberry Touch, I grabbed my white and grey MK print bag and headed out. As soon as I pulled up to Aunt Fi's house, I got out and used my key to let myself in. My babies were on the couch and ready for mommy. I smiled as soon as I saw them.

"Hey my babies," I called as they ran and jumped in my arms.

"Mommy, mommy," they yelled, almost knocking me down.

Sasha's Aunt Fi had been a blessing, because without her I wouldn't be able to go to school, have a life, or even manage twins. She had no problem helping us with the kids, and she has shown me more love than my family over here. My kids are always well taken care of with her. Maybe she doesn't mind because she senses they are related to her. She buys them as much stuff as she does KJ, and they always come home with new clothes on. Today Janai had on a pink tu-tu skirt with a white shirt with pink letters that say Princess by Guess and a pair of all white Uptowns. Her hair was braided up into two ponytails with clear and white beads on them. JJ had on a pair of plaid Polo shorts with blue, yellow, red and green in them, and a white Polo shirt to match. On his feet, he had on some red wallaby Clarkes. His braids were braided to the back and hung past his shoulders. He had my good hair and that made his braids long. I thought about giving him dreads or twists like his dad, but then they would look like twins, and people would definitely know they belonged to him.

I'd never really told anyone the twins are Jyion's, except Sasha. But I guess if you look you can tell, because they have all of his features and my skin tone.

"Thank you for watching them and you need to stop buying them all these clothes and stuff. They're going to be spoiled," I thanked Aunt Fi as I grabbed the kids' book bags.

"Treajure, I love when the kids are here. Besides, they need you focused on school and I'm sure once their daddy finds out about them, I won't be able to steal them away anymore," she said, giving me a hug and a look that told me she knew they are Jyion's kids. "Treajure, you cannot hide them forever. They should be around their father, and they need him."

I wanted to be rude and tell her to mind her own business, but I knew what she was saying was true and I was raised to not disrespect my elders.

"I know," was all I said as I walked out with a lot on my mind.

Strapping the kids in their car seats, I handed them each a toy from the colorful bags on the back of the seats and got in to drive. I figured I would just go to Henrietta Mall because it's closer to the house, in case the kids fell asleep in the stroller. They could walk, but I liked using the stroller to hold my bags. Plus, when you got two little ones running in different directions, it gets crazy. Pulling up to the Old Navy entrance, I popped the trunk, only to see the stroller was not in there. Damn, they'll have to walk. Throwing two juice boxes and pull ups in my purse, I grabbed the kids and while holding each one's hand, I made my way into the store.

Stopping at Finish Line first. I bought the kids the new Jordan's and some sandals for summer, then I went to H & M to grab them some clothes. I had to get a little shopping cart from the store since I was buying so much. They had the cutest little clothes for them and the prices were reasonable.

When She's Your Everything

"Mommy, toys. I want a toy," cried Janai when she saw the little section of toys that every store these days seems to have.

"No, we are here for clothes, Nai, not for toys; you have enough toys at home."

Of course, saying that to a two-year-old is a joke, and as soon as I took my hand off of her and grabbed these white jeans I wanted for JJ off the mannequin, Janai was off and running towards the toys. Grabbing JJ's hand and running after her, I stopped in my tracks so fast JJ fell on his behind and started crying. Picking him up, I called to Janai.

"Janai, come here, right now. You should not run away from mommy. It is not ok."

Janai hadn't just ran away from mommy, but she ran right into her daddy. Seeing her standing so close to Jyion, there was no mistaking that was his kid and I guess the girl with him felt the same way.

"Jyion, what the fuck? I thought this was your first baby that I'm carrying and now I see two kids that look just like you? I'm not taking care of no little brats. Did you see how she was running around the store all alone? No home training," she started talking shit and pushing him on his arm and chest.

Noticing Jyion had a bunch of girl baby clothes in his hands, I felt like someone took a knife to my heart. Damn, him and this girl are having a baby together. She even has a ring on her finger, so I guess they're getting married, too. He killed our first baby, but he's having one with the bitch that Nevaeh beat up at the club. I think she realized who I was at the same time I recognized her, because her facial expression changed to one of rage.

"This is the bitch that was fighting me and my bestie in the club. Bae fuck her up. She was fighting your pregnant fiancée," she demanded as Jyion just stood there holding onto Janai's arm, looking into her dark eyes that mirrored his own. As if in slow motion, he put the baby clothes to the side and picked her up in his arms, holding her close. Surprisingly, she didn't cry. Instead, she popped her thumb in her mouth and laid her head on his shoulder. JJ started pulling away from my grip trying to run over to Jyion as well. Twins are really odd. When one was feeling something, the other one picked it up right away.

Looking back over at this ratchet bitch, I knew she was going to be the migraine of this lifetime.

"Bitch look, you will never be around my fucking kids. They have a mama, so you're out of luck buttercup. And I didn't fight your ass one bit, my friend did after you spilled a drink on her on purpose. Since you want to tell lies and act like you hold some space in Jyion's life, why did he take me home that night and not you?"

Picking up JJ again, I saw her swing on me out of the corner of my eye. Setting my son down, I turned like a fucking ninja and blocked her, then punched her in the nose one good time. I guess this broke Jyion out of his trance, because he snatched her by her throat and pinned her up against a display rack, sending clothes flying all over the place and customers screaming.

"Bitch are you fucking retarded? You didn't see her holding my son when you went to swinging?" he said to her while he was shaking her ass like a rag doll, so I don't know if he wanted her to respond or what. I grabbed his arm to stop him, because the people in the store where staring and he was still holding my baby. He gave me the look like I was next, but hearing Janai whimper he dropped his baby momma to the ground and turned to me.

"Treajure, I didn't know you hated me enough to hide my kids from me all this time. Shit, how old are they? Three? I don't even know their names. I bet they won't go another day without me, so you better get used to my face. Take them home and wait until I get there. I'm coming to spend some time with my kids."

He snatched JJ from me and held both of his kids close, whispering something in their ears. Handing me the kids back, he reached in his pockets and handed me some money.

"Go buy them the shit they need and get to your fucking house. Don't play with me Treajure, because if I have to come and find you, I'mma fuck you up. Text me your address and get my kids in the damn house."

Grabbing the money and going to the checkout, here goes this dumb bitch he fucking wit' talking shit again.

"Yea bitch, you better do as my man says or I'mma whoop your ass. Old dark skin monkey looking ass hoe. Jyion, why you let her hit me? I'm pregnant with your child, those kids are probably not even yours anyway."

Shaking my head, I decided to be a lady and keep walking. I couldn't help but laugh when Jyion spoke again.

"Tauni, shut the fuck up and don't call my baby moms ugly. And on your life, don't ever mention my kids again. Again are you a retarded, bitch? You attacked her first, and besides she hit you in the face and your face ain't pregnant."

He ended the conversation and walked away from her towards the exit with his fists balled up.

Fuck fuck fuck! This is not how I wanted things to go at all. I took out my phone with my hands shaking and texted Jyion my address. I sent Sasha a message telling her to call me when she can. I'd been trying to talk to her the past few days, but she barely called back and she sounded strange when we did talk, rushing me off the phone and shit. I didn't know what was going on, but ever since I found out she was with Ajay, she's been acting distant. I'mma just go over there and sort this shit out as soon as I get done fixing this mess with Jyion's crazy ass.

"Mommy, is that daddy?" JJ asked as we walked to the car. I didn't know how to answer. I guess I couldn't hide this anymore. They'll have to know about their father, because now that he knew, he wasn't going away.

"Yes, JJ and Janai. That's daddy. Did he tell you that?" I asked and they nodded their tiny heads yes. "Ok let's go grab Burger King, and you can have a milkshake and go home so daddy can come see his babies."

I felt like I was trying to calm myself down more than them, because they were babbling in their twin talk and laughing.

Getting the kids some food, I made it home in record time. I expected to see Jyion there already, but I guess he had to finish shopping with his new boo. I mean, the girl was cute but she seemed slack. And what pregnant woman is in the club fighting bitches for no reason. I got the twins settled and decided to call Nevaeh to come over her. Maybe Jyion would show some mercy on my ass with company here, because I saw my kids were already team daddy already.

Chapter 8

Neveah

I left work and decided to go to the park and chill for a while and try to take a quick nap on the bench because I couldn't stand in line for a bed at the homeless shelter until at least 3 p.m. and it was only six in the morning. I was thankful to God I worked overnights three evenings a week and would have a safe, warm, and dry environment for sure on those days. The rest of the week was me barely sleeping on a hard cot with a scratchy blanket of some unknown color and hoping some other homeless person didn't try to steal the little I did have. I don't keep my bank card on me. I lock it up at work and I try to wear my bummy clothes to the mission so people will think I don't have shit. I got shit, just nowhere to put it I laughed to myself as I plopped on the bench and tucked my feet under me propping my chin on my knees. This time of the day is still cold and everything is wet from the early morning dew.

I must have fallen asleep for real because the sun was bright on my face and I could feel my phone vibrating in my pocket. It was Treajure calling. I answered the phone with a silent prayer. I had hoped she would invite me over so I could maybe crash at her house for a little and eat a home cooked meal.

"Hello," I sang into the iPhone trying to sound cheerful.

"Girl, you are not going to believe this bullshit. Remember the girl you fought in the club last week? She is fucking Jyion. This bitch just tried to fight me in the mall with my kids." She got out all in one breath.

"Bitch, wait, where are you? I will come and fuck Tauni up again. You know I got yo' back," I yelled into the phone, already getting off the bench and gathering my stuff.

"Come to the house. I am home now trying to figure out if I should just pack up and move away because Jyion knows about the kids and he is raging mad. I do not want to be around to face him when he shows up. It is going to be ugly."

"Trea, what time is it?" I asked while yawning in her ear

"Shit, did I wake you up? I forgot you work that damn overnight job. Just bring some clothes and come over here for the weekend. I do not want to be here alone when Jyion comes here to *talk*. You want me to pick you up?"

"Naw, I am not far from you. I can be there in about fifteen minutes then I will tell you about this bitch Tauni," I ended the call. I was glad I chose the park near the school so I could go to one of the lockers I use and grab some clothes. I walked up the stairs in the library building. I chose this building to claim two of the big lockers because the library is always open with kids floating in and out so it was not as awkward for me to be here on weekends or nights when I needed my stuff. I still couldn't believe Frank but he will get what's coming to him.

Using the key to the padlock, I unlocked the locker on the far right, number 701. I grabbed my Victoria's Secret duffel bag and shoved in three pairs of clean panties, two pajamas, two sweat suits, and two cute outfits. I was wearing some Old Navy flip flops so I threw a pair of sneakers and two pairs of sandals in the bag as well. Last, my bag of hygiene items and makeup got tossed in. Zipping it up, I threw my book bag over my shoulders and the duffel bag in my right hand and began the walk to Treajure's house. By the time I got there I was sweaty and sticky. Even though it was only early May, the sun was beating down on me and these bags where heavy as fuck.

"Oh my God Nev! Why you look like that? Your hair all sweated out and you breathing all hard and shit. You and Frank was fucking before you came over here or something?" Treajure asked me, joking, as I walked in the front door.

"Ok Miss Nasty, no. Me and Frank broke up a week ago and I walked from the school. I needed a book to study over the weekend and I forgot it in my locker. Can you be a good host and let me take a shower or something? A bitch worked all night and I feel icky, and where the fuck is Sasha ass at because I am only saying this drama about the girl Tauni once."

"Girl, Sasha is MIA since I found out she started fucking with that nigga Ajay for real. It's like he has a hold on her or something, but I am not seeing her like I used too. I left her a voicemail and sent her messages on the book and WhatsApp, so we will see if she responds or just sits up under that nigga," she explained. I just shook my head as I made my way to the guest bathroom to go and take a quick shower.

Wiping the steam from the bathroom mirror, I tried to smile at the face looking back. My sewed in hair was still looking fresh thanks to Sasha, and my brown face was still blemish free but I could see a few worry lines under my pretty, almond shaped eyes. I was too young to be going through all of this but what choice did I have but to keep pushing?

I sat on the couch and waited for Treajure to get comfortable before I started telling her what I knew about Tauni, not bothering to wait for Sasha.

"Ok, so the girl Tauni from the club the other night was my best friend for fifteen years. We went to school together and lived in the same area, all that good shit. When we turned fifteen, she had a baby. Now, I am not knocking anyone who has a kid young, if you handling your business then cool. Tauni did everything but handle her business. She moved out of her parent's house and in with this dude named Reggie. This guy was trying to fuck all her friends and taking all the money her parents gave her to get high. This is what started to mess our friendship up. He kept trying to fuck me every time I came around, and I don't mean just grabbing my ass or something. He was straight up asking me could he fuck and how we could keep it on the low. I don't have time for that nonsense so I stopped coming around only for her to accuse me of trying to sleep with his raggedy ass. I guess the truth hurt so she had to turn it around.

"She never learned, just kept sticking up for him and telling anyone who said otherwise that they were fighting against her relationship and were haters. Eventually he ended up stealing her little Honda and crashing it one night and a few days later she found out he was fucking her other friend, Tracia. After all of that, she finally got rid of him then she began drinking and smoking weed. All her money went to weed and she stayed lit. By the time her daughter, Vicky, was three she had another baby. The fucked up thing was she couldn't take care of either one of them and had no idea who either father was.

"The neighbors kept calling the cops because her kids where found playing outside several times at night. Her daughters were one and three at the time and she took no heed to the cops' warnings about doing better and keeping a closer watch. They even suggested she get a chain lock for the door but that must have been too much effort for her. One day she smoked an ounce of weed that was sprayed with spray paint to get an extra high with her new best friend, the one and only Tracia. The two of them went in the bedroom and began sexing each other. They were so high that they did not even remember that two small kids were in the other room left unattended. The cops found them naked in each other's arms when they woke her up to tell her that Vicky fell out of the kitchen window. A few neighbors were outside when it happened and had tried to encourage the small child to get away from the third story window and go get her mommy when she fell. They said the little girl was acting strange, wobbling around, and mumbling words that made no sense. She had caught a contact high from Tauni smoking in the same room as them earlier in the day.

"Sadly, that was the day I was glad I made a decision to change my circle of friends because that is not what I was about. Shoot, little Vicky just died a year ago and even I could see Tauni had a little belly. I can't believe any nigga would get her pregnant. Shit, I wonder why she isn't in someone's jail cell. I hope that baby is not Jyion's, I mean shit he seems nice and that will be a nightmare he has to deal with for the rest of his life. Know what I mean?"

"So wait, this bitch is a lesbian and doesn't take care of her kids? Naw, my fucking kids won't be going to visit their daddy with that type of girlfriend. I am about to make it clear that when he visits his kids, she has to stay somewhere else or he better visit them at Sasha's house or something," Treajure responded. Her face was turning red under her dark skin and I could tell she was getting pissed. Noticing how quiet it was, I wondered where the kids were.

"Where are the twins?"

"Girl, they are, thankfully, taking a nap for once. I took them to the park after the mall just to wear them out because I knew this shit with Jyion and his new hoe was gonna be stressful. He is really dating this bitch that let her kid die. Basically, she killed her. I guess birds of a feather and so forth and so on. I can't believe him, running over here fucking me and all along he is messing with her too."

"Girl, I am sure he doesn't know shit about that. No nigga want a chick that let their kid fall out of a window. Come one now," I told her, trying to give her a reality check. "You should tell him what's up. If that's his kid she is carrying, he may need to know to keep the baby safe." Rolling her eyes, Treajure jumped up to go check on the kids. I sat back in the couch hoping I could catch a little more sleep but before that dream became a reality the front door flew open and in walked the man I couldn't get out of my dreams. His walk was even sexy but the second he opened his mouth, all dreams went out the window.

"Hey Miss Thot. Whats up? You live in this bitch now? I mean, every time I come here your ass is here with an overnight bag lying in the couch relaxing like this your shit." Tilting his head to the side and staring at me he called out to Treajure, "Trea, this your girlfriend, you like girls now? I get it, that's why she always here like she ain't got no home and shit. Damn, I guess that's why you be treating that dude Lamar like an inconvenience. Ha. Make sure I don't walk in on no girl-on-girl action. I mean, normally I am down but you're like my little sis so that's just nasty."

How can someone so fucking sexy be such an asshole? Not even thinking, I grabbed the closest thing to me, one of KJ's action figures, and threw it right at Covey's face. I hit him above the eye and he had a little cut. I called him a jerk and made my way upstairs with a smile on my face. I almost expected him to come tackle me and kick me in the face or throw me out the front door. A little part of me wanted him to come and chase me to the bed and jump on me. He does pay the rent here so technically this is his shit, but, surprisingly, I didn't hear another word out of him. The last thing I remembered thinking before I fell asleep was that I hope I didn't scar his handsome face.

Chapter 9

Treajure

I waited all night on Jyion to come see the twins and deal with me but he never showed up, so fuck him. I was not going to wait around all weekend long. Nevaeh and I hung out all night watching movies and eating junk food. I had wished Sasha was here-it would have been perfect. Maybe she was hiding from her cousin too.

Lamar had been calling again but this time he was not talking shit-he is apologizing. He had sent a text message saying he was being mean because he thought I was with someone else and he was so in love with me he didn't know how to act. I understood why he thought I wasn't that into him. Shit, I'm not, but the man who has held my heart for all these years has a soon-to-be wife and a baby on the way so I had to make it work as best as I could.

"Nevaeh, you busy tomorrow?" I asked my friend as she looked back at me with narrowed eyes. I knew she was about to talk shit. She really hated Lamar. I think she even said once she wanted him to get killed in the streets. Good thing he is not a street nigga.

"Nope. Why Treajure? What's up?"

"I was wondering if you wanted to hang out with the kids for a little while tomorrow so Lamar can take me out to lunch. Pleeeease! I will let you have the car so you can take the kids wherever you want," I pleaded with her and finally gave her the puppy dog face. Laughing, she nodded yes.

"Not because I want you going out with Lamar but because I miss my little munchkins and we gonna have a blast tomorrow. We hitting the spray park and then the regular park and I am cooking them a nice lunch because we know what happens when you cook."

Giving her the finger, I rolled back over and kept watching the movie. I looked at my phone. I sent Jyion a nasty message telling him thanks for abandoning our kids before I fell asleep mad and disappointed. That was one of the reasons I didn't want to tell him about our kids because he didn't want the first one with me and I guessed he is not interested in these two either, and I not about to let him hurt my kids.

Waking up to kisses from my babies, I got up and smelled something so good I hurried to handle my hygiene so I could go eat.

"Tee Tee Vaeh is making waffles mommy," Janie said with a smile. Shit, I was smiling too. I didn't just suck at cooking, I hated the whole act of cooking. We ate out a lot in this house, but I would rather do that than poison my babies. I talked to Nevaeh over breakfast about school and dumb stuff, and then before I knew it, I had to get ready to go out with Lamar.

Looking in my closet, I found a cute cream skater dress from BeBe that I put on with a pair of gold sandals and gold accessories. I sprayed Moonlight Path body spray on and bounced down the stairs to wait on him to pick me up. I made sure to keep a smile on my face even though I was already annoyed with Lamar and had not even seen him yet. And Jyion had me on a thousand. I tried to always be positive when my kids were around. I guess you can say I had to fake it to make it, but I don't want my bad mood to ever affect them-especially when it has nothing to do with them.

"Damn Treajure your breasts are huge! Did you sneak and get a boob job and not tell us?" Nevaeh teased me. I looked down at my breasts and realized they did look bigger. Come to think of it, they had been tender lately too. Maybe my period was coming on.

"I think it's this new bra I have on, but thanks boo. I am sure Lamar will appreciate it." Hearing the horn blow, I bent down to hug my babies. "Alright, I will be back soon. Their swim stuff is on the bed and I left some money on the table for them to get ice cream or whatever when you guys are out and about. Don't worry. It's Covey's money not mine," I told her as I breezed out of the door.

"Hey babe. You're looking good today. After lunch you need to come ride this dick and show me how much you missed daddy," Lamar said as I climbed in the car.

Turning my head to look out the window so he wouldn't see me rolling my eyes, I dryly responded, "Sure," while he went on and on about the different ways he was going to fuck me and how much he knows I miss it. Honestly, I didn't. He was not a bedroom bully at all. His sex was ok, but not what I dream about at night. Not like sex with Jyion.

"Babe, we still going to the Chinese buffet right?" he asked as he drove that way.

"I would prefer if we went to Red Lobster. I am craving shrimp. I don't know why but I really have a taste for it," I said.

Shockingly, he didn't talk shit. He just made a left on Jefferson and went where I wanted to go. Pulling up at the restaurant, I was suddenly starving and couldn't wait to get inside. Once we'd both ordered, I sat back sipping my fruity drink and decided to try and make conversation with Lamar.

"Babe, how is business going? I need to stop by and grab me and the kids some new sneakers soon." His sneaker store was always busy so I knew it was doing well, but I needed something to talk about and he was kind of boring.

"It's going good. I am getting ready to open a second store on the west side to make it easier for my customers over there. You think I should call it The Spot II?"

My phone started vibrating as soon as he started talking so I was distracted and did not hear what he was asking me. Jyion chose then to call me. Well, sorry. I am not home so you can see your kids another time.

"Yeah babes, that sounds good," I responded not knowing what I'd agreed too. Finally, the food came and I didn't have to keep pretending I cared about what he had to say. The first bite of the shrimp was like heaven. I swear lately food has been tasting better than ever. As soon as I started eating my steamed vegetables I felt a hand on my shoulder. Before he even spoke, I knew who it was from the smell of his cologne.

"Treajure Ann, I guess you don't know what 'take my children home and stay the fuck there until I come' means?" Jyion said while looking down at me like I wasn't sitting at this table with my man. He had the nerve to have his face all bawled up like he and I were together and he had any right to tell me what to do.

"Yo', my man. I don't know who the fuck you are but this is my lady so I suggest you keep it moving my nigga," Lamar said like he was about that life. I didn't know whether to laugh or cry, so I did neither. I just sat there looking at Jyion like he'd had lost his mind. I could have clapped back but today I'mma let Lamar be a man and do what he doing. Feeling my chair being pulled back from the table, I looked up to see Jyion with one hand on my arm helping me up, forcefully.

"My man, no disrespect but this right here is all me and always will be. I understand you had some time wit' her and that's cool, but now I am here so she don't need you anymore. Now Treajure, let's go home so I can spend some time with my kids and I'm not gonna say it again." Throwing a hundred-dollar bill on the table, Jyion began leading me towards the door. I saw Lamar jump up and approach us as he was talking big shit.

"Hey yo' pussy just because you and her got some kids don't mean shit. Like I said this is my bitch and we eating so I'm gonna need you to remove your fucking hand offa her and get the fuck on."

Seeing Jyion's hand move in a flash, he pulled a nine from behind his back and pointed it at Lamar. People in the restaurant started screaming and running as we made our way out the door, this time with me dragging him. I wondered what he was doing here anyway. Well, I guess whoever he was meeting with will be seeing him another time. We made our way to his car, got in, and he began driving to my place.

"Jyion, look I don't know why you drop down in my fucking life and come mess up everything I have going for myself. I don't understand why you just can't leave me alone. You never wanted me before and now you are everywhere- popping up when I am sleeping, eating, and even out with my man."

"Oh that's your boo huh? That why you was sitting at that table looking more in love with that food than his bitch ass. I can't believe you think you can lie to me. First of all, and most important, where the hell are my kids? I know they are not with Aunt Fi because I went over there already. I don't know how you got my whole family hiding my damn kids from me. You really think you are slick huh? I never thought you would be one of those females that would do some evil shit like that."

"Jyion, the kids are with my friend Nevaeh. She loves them and they are out having a park day."

Stopping me before I could really go in on him, "The thot" he asked? I laughed so hard I had to pull my knees up in the car seat and put my face down to get control.

As he pulled up to my house I rolled my eyes at him letting him know I was annoyed that he even remembered where I lived, I jumped out and slammed the door but that didn't stop him from following me as I turned the key in the door. "Look, let's start this shit over. First of all, your cousin Covey is an asshole and my friend is not a thot. He just mad he like her, so he steady talking shit. Told the girl the way her ass jiggles is what makes her a thot." I told him as I threw myself down on the couch.

"Covey ass is wild. He better stop playing before she fuck him up one of these days for calling her names. Anyway, stop trying to change the subject. Call her to bring my kids home and no you ain't fucking wit' Lamar ass. Ole low budget hustling backwards ass dude. If you want to move on, at least go get with a real man and not a lame one," he said with his face bawled up as he made himself comfortable on the other couch.

When She's Your Everything

"You can't tell me who to be with just because I am not about to be wit' you. I am in love wit' Lamar and if he is a lame because he doesn't sell drugs and is an honest business owner, then fuck you. You sit here judging me and have no idea what I have been through. You think raising two kids alone was what I wanted? I tried to call you and you hung up on me. I was here living with my aunt who hated me and her son who kept trying to touch on me every chance he got. I found out I was pregnant with no job and no hope living in a terrible environment. I was scared and all alone. You never came looking for me or cared about me one bit. I had to accept money from Covey to make sure me and our kid were ok, or we would have been living on the streets of NYC, " I yelled, breaking down crying, even though that was some shit I didn't want to do. I didn't want him to see me like this or to know how vulnerable I still was when it came to him, but I just couldn't hold it all in any more.

"Treajure, the love I have for you will never end. I have never turned my back on you. I am sorry I hung up on you when you called. I was mad that you just left and didn't say another word to me. Not a call or letter, nothing in months. But since you think I am so fucked up just know this, this house you living in, that car you driving and that allowance you get every month is all me. I paid for all of this shit. I never left you out. When motherfuckers was telling me to buy you a bucket, I told Covey make sure you got whatever car you wanted. I have never in all these years spent money like that on no bitch. I came here and hit the ground running. I stood on the corner day and night, in the cold or rain selling bags of crack and then bricks until I had enough to make sure you was straight. I did all of that for you, Treajure and never demanded to know where you lived or how you spent the money. All I asked was that you was in school and that you was happy." Getting up and opening the front door, he turned and looked at me one more time.

"Out of respect, please let me know when my son and daughter are home so I can spend some time with them. I don't want to let my kids down." With that he slammed the door and left me sitting there speechless.

Chapter 10

Covey

I threw on my cut off jean shorts, a white and blue V-neck Armani t-shirt, my white and blue Lacoste sneakers then added my iced out Jesus chain with an iced out bracelet to match. Looking in the mirror one more time, I could see my braids were looking fresh and the tattoo on my neck was still looking brand new. I still had a little scratch on my face from that fucking crazy ass Nevaeh throwing the baby's toy and catching me dead in the face. I couldn't even be mad. I mean, shit I guess I was pushing things a bit. I grabbed my blue Yankees fitted and I was ready to go. As soon as I'd made it downstairs, Treajure was giving me the evil eye while talking on her phone to God knows who.

"I hope that ain't bitch ass Lamar you talking too," I said as I grabbed the car keys motioning for her to come on and hoped she would hurry up.

I couldn't wait for her car to come out the shop because me playing chauffer is not the move. I'm about to pay these motherfuckers extra to fix it faster. The reason I got the girls cars to begin with was so I didn't have to drive them from place to place like when we first got here. So when I find out who stole the fucking tires off the car, I'ma break their neck. Like, how shit like that even happen? Treajure went to class yesterday morning and came out to find her 2015 white Nissan Maxima sitting on the ground. All four tires were stolen in broad daylight. I just don't get that shit. It had to be someone she knew. I bet it's that bitch Lamar and when I find out, he is done.

Pulling up to the University of Rochester, Trea jumped out with that heavy ass bag of books in one hand and her purse in the other.

"Covey, I only have one class today so come back in an hour please," she said with a smile. Hell, she didn't even wait for me to say aight or nothing, just gently closed the door to my black Benz still chatting on her phone and skipping down the path. Ha, she is lucky Jyion is out of town with Tauni today or I would send his ass to pick her up.

Instead of hitting the streets the streets for the little time I had, I decided it didn't even make sense so I just parked and chilled in my car for an hour fucking around on the phone with different bitches. As soon as I pulled up to LeChase Hall, I saw Treajure walking towards me only she was not alone. Dragging behind her was her thot friend, Nevaeh, I think her name is. Fuck it, Let me stop lying to myself. I know her name. She is cute as fuck. Last time I saw her in the club I thought I was going to get blue balls just looking at her fat ass and I was getting pissed when all those little niggas were slapping her ass and shit. Looking closely at her, I could see she had her hair in a new shorter style but it fit her face. Today, her face that normally shone, looked almost grey and her shoulders were slumped. Even her one dimple in her cute little chubby cheeks seemed to be hiding. Her nose ring was the only thing shining in the sun light.

"Covey, please drop Nevaeh off. She is not feeling well and I don't want her to fall out on the bus," Treajure pleaded with puppy dog eyes. She and those fucking hazel eyes that made her look so innocent; man I can never tell her no. Her brother was my li'l man and I let him get killed so it was my job to make sure his only sister was straight all the time, even if it meant her ass had become a little entitled in the process. That didn't mean Trea had to know that so thinking of some smart shit to say, I looked up at shorty again and could see she really was sick as fuck. She was leaning against the nearest tree with sweat forming on her face. I jumped out and opened the door then grabbed her book bag from her.

"Get in ma before I have to pick your ass up when you drop. Looking like a vampire who got caught in the sun and shit," I told her, half joking. For once I didn't have it in me to treat her mean. She was looking so pitiful. Staring up at me as I went to close the back door, she gave me a slight smile. I guess she knew it was a joke too.

"Covey thanks so much. She needs to go downtown so just drop me first please because Auntie Fi is dropping off the twins and I don't want her to wait. Plus I am closer," Treajure continued to direct me on shit the whole way to the house. She is a trip. Both she and Sasha are bossy and spoiled as fuck. I guess it's my fault, but shit, they're the only ladies I love so they can have whatever they like. Pulling up to the house to let Trea off, my phone rang back to back. It was this girl I mess with on the regular named Chanel.

"Yo'," I answered her with an annoyed tone. Shit, call me once. If I don't answer, I will call back.

"Hey babe. I was just calling to see what you doing," she answered in response. Looking in the mirror as I made a lane change, I saw Nevaeh in the back shaking and shit. I swear she looked worse than when I picked them up from school earlier. I put the phone on mute when I stopped at the red light and turned around to get a better look.

"Hey ma, you aight back there?" I asked her with worry. She opened her mouth to speak but nothing came out so she just nodded her head. I turned my attention back to a screaming Chanel. All I heard was something about Michelle seeing me with a girl that is not one of my sisters and some other bullshit.

"Covey are you listening to me?" she began to yell in my ear.

"Actually Chanel, I ain't listening. Look I'm busy I'ma hit you back in a while." Not waiting on a response, I pressed the red end button and threw the phone in the seat knowing I wasn't calling her retarded ass back until I needed my dick licked on. Once I hit Main

Street, I wasn't sure where to go. "Yo' ma, what street you live on?" I asked her.

"You can let me off right here." She struggled to get out. I was a little skeptical because I mean shit, Main Street itself is all buildings, no houses or apartments really so where is she going? I asked her again if she was sure. She nodded and opened the door. I watched her slowly struggle with her bag while she walked down the street and it kind of pulled at my heart. There was something about this girl. That is why I tried to stay away from her ass. I didn't have time to be chasing behind any women or catching feelings for one. I had to focus on making this money. Plus, I knew how these females were and you really can't trust them.

Watching Nevaeh slowly walk down the street, I realized I was still pulled over for some reason just sitting there. She seemed to just stop. Thinking she was too sick to walk farther, I sped down the road a little. What the fuck? I didn't even know how to respond to the shit I was seeing. Nevaeh was standing in the line at Open Door Mission, a fucking homeless shelter. She was in line behind a creepy looking baldheaded cat that looked like his drug of choice was crack. He kept turning back to look at her and then he groped her fucking breast. Shit, I couldn't even let shorty go out like that. What is she even doing here any fucking way?

"Yo' man, keep yo' fucking hands to yourself my dude," I yelled as I jogged over to the line shoving him so hard he fell in the street and his body hit the curb with a crunch. I was illegally parked on

West Main but fuck it, I didn't even care. I didn't have any drugs on me so it was what it was. Grabbing baby girl by the arm, I shoved people to the side and walked her back to my whip.

"Covey, what are you doing? I know how you feel about me so there is no need to feel sorry for me. I can't mess around and miss my place in line. They fill up quick and I need a bed to sleep in tonight, as you can see," she said in a panicked voice.

For once in my life I didn't have shit to say, no smart ass comment or even a solution to her problem. This was some shit I would have never expected from her.

"Yo', how long you been living this way? Do the girls know?" I had to ask. I mean, she was young and hot but she was living on the streets. I didn't get it. I even remember Sasha saying she got a job so what was she doing with her money? She didn't look like a crackhead but these days you can never fucking tell.

Moaning for a few minutes as I shoved her in the back seat of the car, she finally answered me.

"Covey, no the girls don't know and please don't tell them. I wasn't always homeless and yes I work, but I also have to pay tuition for school and that consumes most of my funds. I am an orphan so I do not have any family and I have to survive the best I can," she spit out, stopping to cough for a few minutes. Damn, li'l mama sounded terrible. I was going to take her to my house but I was beginning to wonder if I should be taking her to a hospital or some shit instead.

"So what happened to the spot you had before this shit happened? You couldn't make the rent?" I asked.

"I used to live with my boyfriend. His name is Frank and we had been together for four years since high school. One day I came home to find my clothes on the front steps and the locks changed. I was lost as fuck even with his little text saying he knew I was calling his mom and telling her that he was beating on me and that he was stealing from his job. I didn't know what was going on. I didn't even speak to his mom unless it was an emergency because she didn't like me and he had never had a real job. After waiting around for a while across the street, I finally saw the real reason he'd kicked me out. He pulled up with a girl in a maxi dress and a big ole pregnant belly. Helping her in the house me and him once shared, I realized he moved his side chick in and threw me out. I ran over there to fuck up both of them only to find out that not only was she pregnant, they had a two-year-old son." She finished her story with so much sadness in her voice I wanted to reassure her or something.

Pulling off Main Street, I had to think about my next move. I usually didn't bring any females to my crib but I didn't think she was going to make it in a hotel with how she was looking. I made a U-turn then hopped on the expressway going towards Pittsford. I got off my exit and headed down a quiet street lined with trees. I pulled up to my house. I lived way out in the best suburb they got up here. I do a lot of shit in the streets, not just selling drugs, so I like to be out of the way of all of that. Looking back at Nev, she was curled up in a ball sleeping like a baby. Her pretty face was only interrupted by the huge rings around her eyes and the pale hue her skin had from being sick. I bet she got sick from being exhausted. I am sure she was not sleeping like that in the homeless place. Shoot, look at the guy who was fucking with her. There were probably a bunch of creeps in that place waiting to fuck with her.

I pulled up to my house and waited for the garage to open so I could pull in. Damn, I thought I knew that nigga Frank too. If he is the short fat brown nigga who drives a red Lexus, I definitely knew that nigga. He cops weed from me and I always see him with a different bitch. Hell, I used to think that shit was funny but not so much now. And if it is him, he has a lame ass excuse for kicking shawty out since he can't be stealing from a job he doesn't even have. And it's not her fault you got a side baby mom. He should have been a fucking man and just moved out. The thing that threw me off was that I actually believed ma and what she told me. Just like that, I couldn't keep fighting the fact that this girl interested me, even though I really didn't have time to be getting attached to any chick. I still have unknown enemies out there I have to find and I had a feeling they were closer than I wanted them to be.

Hopping out the Benze, I opened the back door and I grabbed li'l ma's duffel bag and book bag. Man, she must be strong as fuck to be carrying this shit around because the book bag weighed about sixty pounds on its own. I opened the front door and set the stuff down on the hardwood floors. I decided to carry Nevaeh in the house instead of waking her up. As soon as I opened the door and grabbed her in my arms, her skin was burning mine through my clothes. Damn, she has a fever and is even shaking in my arms. I only knew a little bit about taking care of someone who is sick so I was not sure what to do. I decided to Google some shit. I took out my iPhone and looked up what to do for someone who is running a fever. They said I should take her temperature first. Fuck, I don't have anything to do that with up in here.

I decided to wipe her down with a cool cloth, give her some Tylenol flu pills, and some lemon grass tea. Tea helps everything so I knew she would be feeling better soon after, at least I hoped she would. I laid her on my bed, removed her sweat pants, then her matching t-shirt. She had on a light blue thong with a matching lace bra. Her skin was flawless. In Jamaica we would say her skin is clean. No marks or cuts anywhere, she had the cutest beauty mark on the inside of her left thigh. Not being able to help myself I leaned down and kissed her in that same spot. I swear I heard her pussy gush a little so I backed off. I wasn't the kind of nigga who took advantage of anyone while they were sick and shit.

As soon as I got her cleaned up, I slid one of my white tees on her and laid her in my bed. She seemed to be doing a little better since the medicine. I watched her slowly sip her tea and look at me with her eyes half closed. I felt uncomfortable, this right here was too intimate, I am not used to having a female in my space. Hearing my business phone ring, I was happy to answer.

"Yo' whats good?" I asked this young nigga named Man who worked for me.   "Everything is cool. I got some cookies for you when you have time," he told me talking in code. Cookies meant money-my fucking money-and I am always happy to come through and collect that. I moved hard in these fucking streets because I didn't have a choice. I am the oldest and I have a lot of people depending on me.

"Aight cool. I'mma come through and hit you up soon. Don't move," I commanded then hung up before he could respond.

"Hey ma, look I gotta make a run fast and handle some business. You gonna be good until I get back?" I asked her, not wanting to really leave her alone because she was not feeling well, but I am a nigga who is about his paper and I don't let anyone get in the way of that. She slowly nodded her head ok and gave me a pained smile.

"Covey, I can have Treajure come get me. I heard you on the phone with her earlier and I don't want to inconvenience you."

I didn't want to let her go so I lied, "You are straight here and anyway, Trea didn't get her car back yet. They found some other shit wrong with it." Walking out of the bedroom door, I turned around to get one more look at her before I left. She had spread out in my bed on her stomach. Her hair was covering half of her face and her body rose and fell with her light breathing. Damn, I have to get her out of my system and fast. This was not what I signed up for.

Rolling up to the apartment near downtown, I sent a text letting Man know I was here. He was this mixed dude who copped a few pounds of weed from me at a time. I gave him half this time on consignment and I am happy to see he is about his money because he got mine and enough to re- up.

"Hey man, everything alright?" I asked as he hopped in the car.

"Yeah man, I am good. Here is the bread and I will send you the address I am using for the next shipment," he said as he exited the car just that fast. I looked around the parking lot before pulling off. I circled the block a few times making sure no one was following me and once everything looked clear, I headed home.

As soon as I walked in the door I smelled something cooking, it was so good my stomach made a noise that I knew Nevaeh could hear in the quiet house.

"Covey, I am sorry that I just helped myself to your kitchen but I wanted to make you something for dinner as a thank you for taking me in for the day. I called Treajure and she is picking me up tomorrow. I already feel so much better because of you," she said, sitting on the chair at the kitchen bar wearing my t-shirt and a pair of spandex shorts she must have had in her bag.

"Shit, it's cool ma. What you made? I hope you don't cook like Treajure or I'ma have to pass," I told her being dead serious. For Christmas, I am getting little cuz some cooking lessons before one of us ends up dead fooling with her. Some people just cannot get down in the kitchen-even if they try. Her laugh was still kind of weak but it told me she was also experienced chef de la Treajure. I wonder if she was eating well enough while she was living on the streets. That could be another reason why she was sick. Washing my hands, I set down at the breakfast bar across from her and waited for my plate. Honestly, I don't know what she found to cook in this bitch because I barely eat here or have any food. Maybe one of the girls bought some groceries when I wasn't around. Treajure can't cook but sure as hell knows how to shop. Sometimes Aunt Fi comes over here and cooks Sunday dinner. She was in love with my kitchen, so it had to be one of them.

When she set a plate of shrimp, white rice, and asparagus with a cheese sauce on top in front of me, I was impressed. The food smelled so good and once I'd started eating, it was damn good.

"Aight ma. You cute, you smart, you can cook, and you got the thot jiggle, but you were fucking with ugly ass Frank? I am lost as a motherfucker. Like, did you not see this nigga big belly when you cuddled up to him at night or tried to give him a hug?" I had to raise my eyebrows when asking her because I was not joking and I wanted an answer. That nigga was ugly as shit.

"Covey, looks are not everything. People gain weight sometimes, but you just don't leave them or turn your back on them. I knew Frank for a long time and the belly came with age. I thought of him as someone who loved me understood me and who would protect me, so no matter what he looked like, I was loyal to him. I loved him. Feelings cannot be changed by looks or money or any other thing like that."

"Well, damn, I wish I could find a girl that loyal. Although look at where that loyalty got you, out on your ass. I need you to get a backbone ma. Don't let any man play you. I better not see this shit happen again. I know someday you are going to be a great one for someone who actually deserves you," I told her as I grabbed the plates and took them to the sink. I guess I will wash them. Shit, I hadn't washed dishes in years but she was wilting again and should probably lie back down. Talking about she feel better. Ha.

"Wait. Covey, how do you know what Frank looks like?" she asked with a panicked look in her eyes. Maybe she thought this was all part of Frank's game or some shit. She was looking like this nigga was hiding in my closet or under the table.

"Nev, me and frank are not friends or anything. I just know him from business. Trust me, I don't fuck wit' him like that and I don't approve of how he treated you. I would never treat a girl like you the way he did. Come on, you looking sick all over again let's get you back to bed." I motioned to her as I walked towards the master bedroom.

"Umm, what room do you want me to sleep in because I think I was in your bed earlier, and since you are home now you have to sleep somewhere so I can go to a guest room or even the couch if you would like," she stuttered in her little sweet voice.

"Naw, go back to the bed you were sleeping in, the guest rooms have no furniture and I don't want anyone sleeping on my couches creating dents and shit."

As soon as we got to the room, she climbed in bed looking unsure as hell, especially when I started taking off my clothes. Throwing on some polo shorts with no shirt, I could see her eyes lingering on the tattoos on my chest then moving down to my washboard flat stomach and began looking even lower. I climbed onto the bed next to her and grabbed the remote right out of her hand just to fuck with her.

"Covey, really? I am watching this show and I am sick, so don't be mean." She pouted talking about some wedding show. Hitting the on demand button and picking a new comedy to watch, I pulled her next to me and smoothed her hair away from her face. I was glad to see she just went with the flow and started watching the movie.

We laughed and joked the whole time and she was struggling to keep her eyes open before the end.

"It's ok, Nevaeh. I know you can't hang ma so just go on 'head and get some sleep." I grabbed the second blanket from the end of the bed and covered her up. I always wondered why this shit had two blankets. I let Trea and Sasha decorate my house so I really don't know what half this shit is for.

"Covey, you not going to your bed?" she asked me.

"Shit, I am in my bed. I told you I don't have any guest rooms set up." For whatever reason, I was lying to stay next to her. I enjoyed being in her presence so I was going to keep her in my space as long as I could.

I climbed under the blanket next to her and pulled her a little closer to my body. Not enough that she would feel how hard she made my dick though. I didn't want to scare her little ass. Feeling her breathing even out as I watched Sports Center, I thought she was asleep until she spoke again.

"Covey, I know Treajure got her car back today. She brought me the groceries and gave me a tour of the house showing me all the other bedrooms, with furniture in them." Just like that huh? I guess she was on to me after all.

Chapter 11

Sasha

Today was the first day in a long time I woke up with another man on my mind who was not Kaneil. Accepting that he was gone forever was the hardest thing I had to deal with in my life so far. I tried not to think about the days when we had a relationship, when he was here to hold me, and make me feel safe and special. I had known Kaneil for a long time because his sister was my best friend and he and my brother were always together. I always thought he was a pain in the ass to be honest. He was so damn pretty and really loved himself to the point it made a lot of people not like him. Also, he was a player so I knew that talking to him would really get me nowhere. But one day we ended up alone at his house while I was waiting on Treajure to get there, and we just started talking. I got to know the real him, the one who was funny and kind and we just clicked. One day he asked me to be his girl.

I'd always thought he was cute but that he would never look at me because he really could get any girl he wanted and he ran through a lot of them. Plus, I was younger. I was flattered and gave him a chance because I really liked him. He was sexy, sweet, and good at sports. I'd always thought he would go to the Olympics or be picked up by a team in the US or England and we would have a bright future. But in the long run all the different girls in and out of his life made it hard for us to focus on the future. I was so in love with him, but he just couldn't leave the girls alone-or he just wouldn't. I had females fighting me on the way home from school, coming to my house looking to beat me up over him, and even some tell me he already had a girl.

When I got pregnant, things actually got worse instead of better. He was gone all the time and had started robbing people for money and drugs. He used the excuse he was broke and had to make a way for the baby and me, but his wild behavior was no good for anyone-especially our baby and me. The day before he was murdered we argued about this girl named Alona who kept calling his phone in the middle of the night and all throughout the day. He told me it was nothing and she was handling some business for him, but I could tell he was lying. I'd told him I hated him and he left my house mad. I never saw him again. He never knew we were having a boy, and I never got to tell him I loved him one more time.

I have had such a hard time getting over Kaneil. The fact that I woke up this morning with a smile on my face thinking about sexy ass Tavian threw me all the way off. Who would have ever thought I would be thinking about another pretty boy ass looking nigga? The only difference is Tavian is not like Kaneil was. Tavian keeps himself up but has never cared much about how his hair looks or if his clothes are matching. However, Kaneil used to be in love with himself. He loved looking at himself any chance he got and spent more time in the mirror and bathroom than his mom and sister combined. Hell, I go through that same stuff with Ajay's ass and he is dark skinned. Maybe it's the kind of men I attract. Yeah, he is sexy with his super cut body and smooth chocolate face, but the feelings I once thought I had for him are dying a slow death because his behavior is ugly. Why do I attract men who care about themselves more than me?

Stretching and allowing my smile to slowly fade, I looked at my phone to see if my no good man had called or texted. I saw nothing from the supposed man I have who didn't know how the fuck to come home or let a bitch know he was not going to be here. Or, maybe he can offer up one of his lame ass excuses like how he was working or handling business. After the incident with my son being hurt by those mice, he came crawling back saying his ex is stalking him and she did that shit to get back at him for being with me. He claimed she broke in the house and even had a bitch call me and tell me the same story and apologize. He even went so far as to file a police report on this bitch. The girl did sound crazy over the phone and he had his act together for a whole week before he started his nonsense again. Now I wish I would have stood my ground and made him get out.

I continued to check the rest of my phone and noticed a few alerts from the 'book and a good morning text from Tavian. Immediately answering Tavian with a morning greeting and a smiley face, I decided to scroll through my other alerts. Tavian had really been there for me since he came back into my life and I couldn't deny the attraction I had for him. I just didn't know how to handle it. I noticed three messages from 2 a.m. I hurried and opened them wondering who in the hell had messaged me that time of the morning.

Goddess Bionca: Hey girl, come and get your husband out of my bed, I am tired of arguing with him and he keeps putting his hands on me. Not even my daddy can put his hands on me. I am a grown ass woman.

Me: Little girl stop playing in my messages and grow up. You are probably some bitch he turned down and now you mad. I know how you thirsty bitches get down and from the looks of your profile picture you have to be one of them.

Goddess Bianca: I'mma show you a turned down bitch wait on it dumb hoe, Ajay Ladell Jones is definitely known over here. When he gets home, I hope you can get the lipstick stain out of those bright green and white polka dot boxers he got on.

Closing out the social media app, I began feeling sorry for myself for being in this relationship. I wanted to call Trea and Neveah but I decided to keep this shit to myself and be a big girl. I had to learn to handle shit alone and not run to a friend, or my brother and cousins, or even Tavian. I jumped up to take a fast shower. I wanted to be dressed and alert when this pussy showed up. As soon as I finished pulling my neon pink tank top over my head, I heard the key turn in the door downstairs. I didn't even allow Ajay to step foot in the bedroom I was in.

"So, Ajay where you been? As a matter of fact nigga, what boxers you got on?" I yelled snatching his grey sweats down. As soon as I caught a glimpse of green and white I picked up the closest thing I could find, which was the Bible-Lord forgive me. I hit him several times in the face. He just stood there in shock until blood squirted out of his lip like a broken faucet.

"Really Sasha? What the fuck has gotten into you, yo'?" His voice boomed as he went to grab me by my hair. I casually moved two steps to the left and watched him trip over his sweats and land face first on the floor. Grabbing my MK wristlet and car keys, I calmly walked out of the room. "SASHA! You better not fucking leave!" Ajay called out, only to be met with a slam of the front door and my laughter. I hopped in my all white seven series BMW and drove around the corner then pulled back in on our street four cars down from my house. I knew it would be a matter of time before this dummy runs right back to his girlfriend's house and I would be there.   I fumbled to log back into my phone and pull up my messenger. I saw Bionca had sent me a bunch of laughing emoji's. I saw Ajay run out and jump into his Infiniti truck. He never even looked back to see if I was still around. I drove and clicked on this bitche's profile picture at the same time. The phone finally loaded the profile image. Looking at the picture, a brown skin chick who was thick with an odd shaped body, an ok face, and fucked up hair appeared.   *BEEP!* A car blew at me as I ran the red light on Ridge Road, not even paying the road too much attention. I flipped the lady the bird and decided to put the phone down for now so I threw it in the seat.

Not even ten minutes later we pulled into Greece Commons across from the skating rink on Dewey Avenue. Wow, he kept his bitch close to where he and I laid our heads. Seeing the same bushy haired chick from the photo walk out of the door like she was leaving, he jumped out of the car and began arguing with her. As I got out of the car, he decided it was a good time to wrap his arms around Bionca as she began to cry. All I could see was red and I didn't even remember how, but the crow bar I kept in my trunk was suddenly in my hands. "Sorry to break up this happy reunion, but fuck both of you!" I screamed as I hit Bionca several times quickly in her legs, side, and back with the metal weapon in my hand. I felt Ajay's strong arms yanking me off the step and then snatching the crow bar out of my hands. I turned to face him. He began to speak first.

"What the fuck is wrong with you shorty? Can't you see she is pregnant and you could have hurt our baby? And I am sure a neighbor called a cop by now and I am not bailing your dumb ass out of prison!" he shouted as he walked over to the screaming Bionca who was balled up in the fetal position rocking her body on the ground.

Wow, a baby. I couldn't believe I didn't notice the big ass belly the girl had. She looked like she was going to have the baby now. I didn't even have any words left for this nigga. I walked over to him and I spit in his face then skipped down the walkway back to my car. Wiping off the side chick's blood on my black leggings, I jumped in and drove back to the house. Now it was time to get the girls on the phone because I had a feeling we were going to have to fuck this nigga up again. As soon as I walked in the room, I dialed and put my phone on speaker.

"Hello," Trea answered.

"Hey sis. Call Neveah on three-way so I can tell you the bullshit this nigga Ajay has been around here doing." I reached under the bed to take out my lock box and find the card with the complex's number so I could change the locks. I spotted one of Ajay's iPhones just lying there from when he fell, looking like a present at Christmas time. I didn't even bother with the unlock shit. I told Siri to take me to his text messages from Bionca. The screen opened up and I was able to see a whole lot of shit I had never wanted to see. Pictures of her in her panties, she and him kissing, and wait, what the fuck is this-a video?

Not even finishing the whole story I cut Treajure off mid question.

"Umm, I have to go right now. I will call you back." I hung up and turned my phone off. I clicked on the video. I saw what looked like a cheap and dingy motel room then soon realized it was this bitch's house. Seeing my man's dick come on the screen and hearing his voice,

Baby come on wake up for me, you know what I want, I could't help the river of tears that began to course down my cheeks. Damn, I knew I wasn't in love with this nigga but I was still with him and I was a good woman. I had never cheated or anything-even when I'd had the chance. Seeing Bionca roll over out of her sleep and begin slobbing on Ajay's dick, I felt disgusted. I wanted to stop watching but I couldn't. My hands began to shake as my eyes didn't even blink looking at this shit. It hurt but it felt freeing because this man who talked down to me, hurt me, and bullied me will have to exit my fucking life after this shit. To make matters worse, he snatched her by her waist and stuck his dick directly into her pussy. No condom, not a piece of protection, and began fucking away. Hearing him say he loved her, I couldn't take anymore. I quickly forwarded the video to myself then threw the phone against the wall, smashing the screen.

I turned my phone back on and called Tavian to see if he was in town, but got no answer. I shot Treajure a text to let her know I would be on my way over after I stopped to pick up Kaneil Jr. from my aunt's. And that I was finally leaving punk ass Ajay alone.

My phone rang with a number I didn't recognize but I answered it. Hearing Ajay's voice far away, I realized he let his bitch get my number from his phone somehow. Since when do these niggas allow their side bitches to do main bitch shit? I focused on his voice and couldn't believe what I'd heard.

"Bionca, I am so sorry baby. You know me and her broke up. I just come around for my son. I am so happy our daughter is ok and I can't wait to hold her in my arms." On and on he went with the lies. This joker and I don't have a fucking kid together and he has nothing to do with my son so what the hell is he talking about? Hearing breathing near the phone I made sure Bionca's ass heard me loud and clear.

"Hey Miss Porn Star, get ready to be internet famous."

Laughing, I hung up and put my plan into place. I knew the video would be removed sooner than later. I also knew that thousands of people would view it before any admins removed it or it was reported. I pulled out my iPad and sat on the edge of the bed and made fake profiles then shared the video of Bionca and my man fucking on every social media site I could find. I even posted that shit to LinkedIn in case she ever needed a job that's not on her knees. Feeling satisfied, I packed an overnight bag and made my way to go have a girl's night with my bestie.

Chapter 12

Treajure

There must be something in the water today. First I get a call from Jyion saying he was locked up for trying to sneak into Canada. What the fuck was he trying to do going into Canada anyway? He knows he doesn't have the right paperwork. So I had to go to his house and meet a locksmith so the locks could be changed because he swears Tauni set him up and he wants her out of his place now. I got up and threw on some black tights and a white tank top. I put my hair back in a ponytail and walked out of the door. He was lucky I was a nice person because all I wanted to do was sleep, and he got my ass out of bed handling his business. As soon as I walked outside, I wanted to turn right back around. Standing in front of my house, leaning on his car, was Lamar.

"Treajure, where the fuck you been?" he asked as he jogged over to me. "You don't hear me talking to you? You just come in and leave our date with some random nigga and then you ignore all of my phone calls?" Rolling my eyes, I kept walking to my car until I felt myself being yanked by my ponytail. This dummy just pulled me by my hair, what the hell?

"Lamar, you must be fucking slow. I like you but this is not a good time for me and you, and I need to be alone. I did send you a message letting you know not to call me anymore and now you show up here acting like a small child."

Tightening his grip on my hair, he moved closer to me licking on my neck and breathing in my ear.

"Treajure, I am not letting you go, so you need to get that through your head. You shouldn't have played with my feelings because you will be punished for that. Be ready for me when I call." He let me go so fast I almost fell to the ground. He calmly jogged back to his car and drove away. Great. Now I have a crazy ass ex-boyfriend.

Getting in the car and driving to the address Jyion gave me, I had reached for my phone to call Sasha but she called me before I could press the button.

"Hey Sasha, what's up?" I figured I would let her talk first since she called me.

"Treajure, I am coming over there because I am going to kill Ajay. He is a snake and I am done with him. As soon as I am done with this, I will be there." All I heard after that was screaming in the background.

"Sasha, are you ok?" I yelled into the phone.

"That's not me. I will be there soon. I need both hands right now." She ended the call with that because then I was listening to a dial tone.

Luckily, I didn't run into Tauni at Jyion's house. I'd had enough confrontation for one day. Riding down the quiet street, I pulled up to the number I had scribbled down on the sheet of paper. It looked nice from the outside. I think it's called a split-level and it was painted green with large windows in the front and bushes and flowers surrounding the house. The locksmith was waiting on me as soon as I pulled in the driveway. All I had to do was grab the new keys and turn around to go home and get back on my couch. I pulled up to my place and held my mace in my hand as I walked to the door in case Lamar decided to pop back up.

Once I'd made it inside, I began looking through some of my alerts because they had been going crazy the whole time I was driving. I noticed Covey had called me like five times. I hurried to call him back. Shit, I'd forgotten I'd asked him to drop off Nevaeh earlier and had asked if she was ok since she wasn't feeling well. Listening to the ringing on the other end, I was hoping she didn't throw up in his Benz or no crazy shit. I also hoped he didn't treat her like an asshole because she really looked awful. Lately, she must have been working a lot of overtime or something because she had been looking exhausted and was never around. I caught her sleeping in our seminar class the other day and I was shocked because Professor Lee is a real bitch. If she saw you sleeping, you were leaving her class for the day.

Answering his phone loud as always, Covey started talking shit right away.

"Yo' let me fucking tell you about your girl. You know she is homeless and shit? I mean, damn, why you ain't ask her to stay wit' you for a while? Did you think I was going to talk shit or something? I mean, I ain't wit' no nigga moving in but this your girl and she is sleeping outside and at homeless shelters and shit." Covey started in on me about something I had no idea was even going on.

"Covey, what the fuck are you talking about? First of all, you hate my home girl and second, what do you mean she is homeless? She has a place of her own on Lime Street. I know the area is not the best at all but she keeps the place nice on the inside. I have been there a few times," I responded, baffled by what the fuck he was talking about.

"When was the last time you were there because trust me, shorty is homeless as fuck. I caught her waiting in line at Open Door Mission downtown and believe me, this wasn't no attention grabbing shit. She is so sick she can barely stand up. I took her home wit' me because I can't have her out here wit' nowhere to go and she look like she gonna die and shit. Once she gets better, man you or Sasha need to help her out. I know I called her names but I think she is a good girl. I checked up on her after she hit me in the face with that fucking toy and I haven't heard anything bad so just be a friend and help her out and shit."

"Aight, I really didn't know. I feel so bad now. As soon as the kids get here I will come and get her. Don't do anything to my friend

Covey!" I yelled before he hung up in my ear. See, it's a full moon today. What the fuck? All this time my girl been homeless. I feel awful for not seeing the signs earlier. She was always asking to take a shower and falling asleep lately when she visited but I didn't think anything of it because she works overnights. Even stranger is the fact that Covey didn't leave her ass right in the line at the shelter, or at the very least drop her on my doorstep in a sick heap and drive away. Maybe she is breaking down the ice around his frozen heart.

Ding. My phone went off with an alert for my Facebook account. I opened up the app and scrolled through my latest messages and tags. I saw Sasha had tagged me and about a hundred other people in a video. I clicked on it and saw a chick with a bad weave and hair tied up in a cheap motel bed. What the heck? Maybe someone had hacked Sasha's account because she was not into posting porn. As soon as the male came into view, I could see her sucking on his little dick, and that was when I saw it. The birthmark I will never forget. It was the same one that the boy had who had tried to rape me as a child. It was shaped like an oval with ridged edges and one side swerved to the right. I will never forget that mark from the day I was more scared than I had ever been. Before I could turn my head, I noticed his face come into view and it was Ajay. What the fuck? All of this time Ajay was one of the guys who had attacked me. That meant he was one of the people who had killed my brother.

With my hand shaking I clicked on the phone icon and dialed Sasha but the phone went straight to voicemail.

"Sasha, hurry up and call me back or get over here. That nigga Ajay is one of the boys who tried to rape me and that means he had something to do with Kaneil being killed. Don't go around him at all. He is sick! Sis call me back asap!" I yelled into the phone before I hung up and put my head in my hands. This was all too much and I thought to call Jyion. Even though we were not on good terms, I know he would want to know this shit.

Hearing the doorbell, I ran and flung it opened thinking it was either Sasha or Auntie Fi dropping off the kids, but instead some lady I had never seen was standing on my doorstep with a little girl next to her. She turned her head towards me when I opened the door and her little braids went flying and the barrettes almost hit her in the eye. The little girl was gorgeous. She had a round baby face, my skin tone, dimples, and my brother's grey eyes. I was so shocked I couldn't even find the words to speak. I felt like my mind was playing tricks on me.

"I am looking for Treajure Palmer. Is she available please?" the lady asked me in a soft tone. Taking a good look at her for the first time, I realized that she was not much older than me and really pretty. She had skin the color of gold with long brown and blonde hair that ran straight down her back. Her brown eyes looked sad and were kind of wide almost in fear. She even looked somewhat familiar, but I couldn't put my finger on it.

"I am Treajure. Is there something I can help you with? I don't believe I know you," I asked, trying to not have an attitude in my voice because I didn't want to scare the little girl who I was pretty sure was my niece.

"I am Alona and this is your niece, Killana, and she is four years old. I am sorry it took me so long to get in touch with you but there were a lot of circumstances that kept me from doing that. I can see the look on your face, but they were truly life or death. My brother threatened to kill someone who is close to you and who was close to Kaneil after h threatened to kill me and my baby. Ajay did not want me to come around because of his obsession with a girl he only referred to as Sasha's friend. Sasha is some girl he dated to get close to her friend and be able to eventually get her to be with him. I guess he has been obsessed with her for years, since we were back in primary school. It is so bad he wouldn't even tell me her name. He just mumbles over and over again that he almost had her once. He ended up with her shirt once. It was a uniform shirt and still had the TGHS pin on it so I knew she went to Tivoli Gardens High School. For some reason the buttons were missing. Anyway, he slept with it for years until my mother threw it away one day thinking it was an old school shirt of mine. He lost it, went so far as to hit our mother with a shoe and run her out of the house. That was the moment I knew he had a problem.

"I know he is crazy but I couldn't wait any longer. My fear is now for my child. My daughter is very sick and she needs a blood transfusion but I am not a match and there is no one else related to her I can turn to. I hope you or your mom would be willing to help, for her sake. I wish I could have met you when Kaneil was alive but he said he was not ready to let his family know about us. He was trying to make some money first before he let them know he had a fiancé and a child. And then, in the blink of an eye, he was gone. So here I am to tell you about Kaneil's daughter and beg for your help. I am sorry I waited so long for you to get to know your brother's only child," she cried, explaining her appearance on my doorstep.

Even though I knew the little girl was his the minute I saw her, I still felt like I was under water and couldn't think straight or form a sentence. My brother had another baby and a fiancé that we had never met or heard of? Why all the lies and secrets and did she say her brother's name was Ajay and that he was obsessed with one of Sasha's friends? What is going on? Had Ajay been after me all of these years and I never knew? Feeling a shiver go through my body I tried to think of something to say but before I could say a word, I looked up and noticed that Sasha was standing behind Alona with tears running down her already bruised face.

"Well, Alona. I am Sasha and I am sorry to tell you, but your daughter is not Kaneil's only child," she said with rage and hurt in her voice as she moved towards Alona. Shit, what do I do now?

Watching in slow motion as Sasha walked up to Alona and grabbed her by her hair, my mouth dropped as she dragged her down the stairs and began punching her in the face and kicking her in the sides.

"Mamaaaa," wailed Killana as she ran right into the fight to try and protect her mother. That is when I moved my ass, putting aside all of the shock of being stalked all these years by Sasha's boyfriend. I jumped down three steps and grabbed my niece. She was precious because she was another part of my brother. My brother who had died because of me. It was all my fault and now he had two kids that wouldn't have a father.

"Sasha stop. This is not her fault. She didn't even know about you and you are going to hurt the little girl," I pleaded with her but it was like she didn't hear me. Holding Killana in my arms now even though she was struggling, I noticed that Alona was not even fighting back. She was just lying on the ground with blood and tears mixing on her face.

Hearing car doors slam I was happy to see that Aunt Fi and Tavian had pulled up at the same time.

"Tav, come and stop this please before the kids see what is going on or Sasha ends up going to jail." He pulled her off of Alona right away and was trying to hold her and whisper something in her ear. Sasha struggled to get free but didn't go for Alona again. Instead, she turned to him and began screaming.

"You don't understand Tavian. You can't make this ok, or anything ok. Kaneil never loved me. I was a joke to him and our son meant nothing. Oh yea, Ajay. I was a fucking joke to him too. He was dating me to get close to Treajure. No one wants me, no one has ever loved me. So no, it will not be alright and I am alone. I have no one and I never will." She broke down crying and sunk to her knees.

"Look, Sasha, I tried to show you how much I love you, have always loved you. But you are still in love with a man who is dead and gone. I don't know what Kaneil's situation was but he is not here, and we always knew Ajay was a piece of shit. So guess what? I am tired of trying. When you stop loving a ghost, call me." Tavian clapped back on her ass, nodded his head at us, and got in his all black Yukon and peeled out. Sasha hopped up and ran to her BMW and did the same.

Helping Alona off the ground, I invited her in so I could help her clean up and calm down Killana.

"I am sorry but someone needs to explain what is going on here," Aunt Fi said as she led all of the kids in the house. I didn't even know where to begin so I started by taking out my phone and texting Sasha that I loved her and that I would keep KJ until she was doing better. No one prepared me for this day. It was not a full moon, it was a damn catastrophe. I hoped Jyion came here when he got out. I needed someone to lean on since my girls were both down and out. Wait, I guess that was what Lamar was for until he'd started acting like a bitch and stole my tires and shit. Yeah, I knew that his ole lame ass had something to do with it. Who else would do that bitch nigga shit? Plus, he knew where I parked my car when I went to class.

I was to the point where I didn't care anymore. Fuck Lamar and Jyion. Jyion is quick to tell me he loves me but then he already has an almost wife and a baby on the way. I know he didn't cheat on me and get together with this girl, but I felt like he did. My heart felt betrayed all over again and I was not going to accept it. The next time he thought he was going to hop on over here for some casual sex, I was going to shut his ass down for real.

Chapter 13

Neveah

Waking up the next morning, I saw that the other side of the bed was empty. If it wasn't for the lingering smell of Covey's Armani Code, I would have thought having him in the bed with me was a dream.

"Covey," I called his name before I got up with the little amount of clothes I had on. Not getting a response, I crawled my way to the edge of the king size bed. I turned the TV on to the music channel and played my jam, *Don't Mind,* by Kent Jones. I went to the linen closet to get clean sheets so I could make the bed. Funny thing is I picked out the red and white polo comforter set I was putting on the bed. When Sasha and Treajure had to decorate the house, I helped them with the shopping. Popping and twerking, I got the bed made in no time. I then took a fast shower, brushed my teeth, and attempted to fix my hair without a curling iron. The house was so quiet so I figured Covey was gone and this would be a good time for me to get out of here. I was so embarrassed that he knew all my business and I didn't want any more pity from him.

I called Treajure again to see if she could come pick me up. I got no answer so I decided to take my chances finding a bus line out here. I grabbed my bags and decided to make Covey some breakfast before I left. I didn't know what kind of females he fucked with but the fridge was empty when I got here until I had Treajure drop off some groceries the other day. Grabbing the eggs, I began making an omelet with cheese, turkey and veggies. Then I made some homemade French toast and bacon. I placed the dishes in the dishwasher and the food in the microwave. I turned around to grab my bags and had my hand on the door when I heard his voice.

"So you were just going to sneak out like a thief in the night?" he asked, staring me down like I was a piece of his breakfast.

"Covey, I can't stay here indefinitely," I simply said, keeping my hand on the door.

"You sure can't" he responded in only that rude ass way he could. Rolling my eyes, I opened the door and had one foot outside when I felt his hand on my arm. "Come on ma, you still a little shaky. Just chill until one of the girls comes and gets you. Hang out wit' me today. We can do anything you want." He coerced me back in the house and snatched my bags up and put them back in the room.

"Ok Covey, let's play games and watch movies, since its whatever I want to do. And, I want pizza for lunch."

Even though he looked at me crazy, he went and got pizza from Pizza Hut and Monopoly and Scrabble from Walmart. And he sat in the living room and hung out with me all day. I could tell it was hurting him to do it, but he even turned off both of his phones and gave me all of his attention. After I whooped his ass in Scrabble for the second time, I was exhausted so I sat my behind on the couch and turned on Netflix. I found the movie *Maid in Manhattan* and pressed play.

"Really B, we watching this girly movie?" Covey talked shit while throwing himself on the couch next to me. Feeling his body close to mine made my heart race and my palms sweat.

"She is really a good mom in this movie," I commented about J-Lo's character."

"Yeah she is, she has a lot against her being a single mom but she takes a chance," he voiced his opinion. It was good to know he respected the struggle women had to face with a kid.   "Covey do you have kids?" I asked on impulse.

"Not yet, just KJ and the twins." He laughed. "Do you want kids someday ,Nevaeh?"

"No, I do not want any kids. I love them but being a mom is not for someone like me." I turned my head so he couldn't see the tears in my eyes.

"Nevaeh, what do you mean someone like you ma? Yo', look at me," he said turning my head. Using his thumbs to wipe the tears from my eyes, he pulled me closer to him. I could hear his heartbeat through the yellow Puma shirt he had on. It was soothing. How do I tell him that I have no one in this world and I don't want to bring up a child that way? I fell right asleep on that couch, in his arms, laying against his chest wetting his shirt with my tears. And just like that, I ended up in Covey's arms in his bed one more night.

I woke up to a surprise. Covey had cooked breakfast for me. It was some fried Plantains, eggs, and vienna sausages. I enjoyed my food while smiling to myself. There was just something about him. He played so hard but was really sweet. He laughed and made jokes but had a serious side. Ever since Covey had taken me home and nursed me back to health, he had not been such an asshole.

I was staying at Sasha's house since she had more space then Treajure and Treajure had Jyion in and out all the time. Even though she was in denial, saying she wasn't fucking with him again, that was a lie. The first two weeks I was here were spent taking care of Sasha since she was heartbroken over Kaneil having another child. I was picking up my keys for a two-bedroom town house in Irondequoit. It was not really near the girls, but this place is brand new and I will just have to pick up more hours at work to be sure the rent is paid. I have to live somewhere so this is it. Plus, if Sasha decides to move, she may want to live out here so I am not all alone.

Covey offered to take me to get my stuff out of storage and the school lockers and bring it in. He also offered to help with the rent and some furniture, but I declined. I had enough from this paycheck to at least buy a bed and some dishes, so that's what I was going to do. He texted me that he was outside and I ran out to his Range Rover.

"Covey, what in the world is all of the stuff in the back of your truck?" I asked, looking behind me at all the Walmart and Macy's bags. I guess he went and got some household stuff or maybe food since I had been teasing him about not having any.

Instead of answering me, he just kept on driving. As soon as we pulled up to my new place, I noticed a huge truck from one of the furniture companies in the space next to mine. Covey jumped out and went to talk to the driver.

"Yo' ma, hand me the keys and start grabbing all the stuff from the back. It's a house warming present from me and the girls." Slowly handing him the keys and grabbing the bags, I went inside. I watched the moving people carry in couches, TVs, a pub table in brown wood with wooden stools and brown leather chairs. Next came beds for both rooms and dressers. I looked in the bags and there were new dishes, towels, shower curtains, and so much more. There was everything a new house needed, even a new vacuum that was hidden under the bags and pillows, sheets, and blankets from Macy's-all in my favorite colors of mint green and pink with splashes of white. I could tell my friends picked all of my stuff, but I think Covey paid for it all.

I stood in the kitchen holding a bag of cleaning supplies and couldn't help but cry because I was so grateful. No one had ever done anything like this for me before.

"Awww, come on Nev. Don't cry, babe." Covey strolled in the kitchen and came closer to me. He leaned towards my face and before I knew what had happened, he'd kissed me gently on the lips. "You deserve this and more. Remember you are special and I got you ma. Don't worry." He kissed me again and then went back to bringing in bags.

I had so much fun setting up my new place and seeing all the things my friends picked out for me. Covey had been coming over since I'd moved in and hung out. Some days he fell asleep in my bed cuddled up next to me, but had not kissed me again and had not tried to have sex with me either. I wished he would do something because I was confused about what we had going on.

I was meeting Sasha and Trea at the mall. I'd decided to wear a summer dress that was red with white flowers on it. I ran my hair through my short cut, threw on a little makeup and some matching white flowery sandals then went outside to get in the car with Treajure.

"Hey boo, you look cute," Treajure told me as I stepped in her car.

"Thanks sis! So do you," I told her and meant it. She was rocking a pair of ripped up Bermuda shorts and a lacy white shirt with white sandals. As soon as we pulled up to the mall, Trea had needed to go to the food court first. She had wanted to eat all the time lately. Seeing Sasha talking to Covey when we walked up, I was so excited to see him.

"Hey Nevaeh, Trea. I gave Sasha some money so you guys can shop and stuff. If you run out, call me," he let us know. He seemed like he was being standoffish. I wanted to hug him but his body language was off. That was when I noticed her standing next to him with her hand on his arm in a possessive manner. She had on black Red Bottoms and a jean dress with tears. It was cute and so was she, except for the pouty look on her face.

I know we'd never said we had anything official, but Covey had said he didn't have a girl but here she was. I felt crushed and just wanted to get away from him and wifey.

"Nevaeh, funny I would see you here. I heard how you were homeless and turning tricks with this nigga right here outside of the homeless shelter so you could have a place to stay. Shit, now that I know you on it like that you can come back home. Remember I got the hook up at the strip club," laughed Frank as he walked up and grabbed my arm. Yanking my arm away, it was just in time for the girl on Covey's arm to punch me in the face. Watching Covey hoping he would save me, he just stood there calling out to her.

"Chanel, let's fucking go man. You are such an embarrassment. That's why I don't take your ignorant ass anywhere," he yelled while grabbing her as she called me a home wrecker and a bitch. Watching Frank laugh so hard as he was holding his fat ass belly, I was crushed all over again. I guess none of these men were shit.

"Nev, I caught that bitch in the back of the head two good times, man fuck her. Chanel is just some bitch he fuck wit' from time to time, nothing serious. Let's go shopping. I got one of Covey's Amex cards. We can shop on that," Sasha said, putting her arm around me and leading me towards the food court once again.

Chapter 14

Sasha

I woke up today and decided that I was giving men a break. I needed to take some time out for myself and my son. I was too young for all of these shenanigans and hurt feelings. Plus, I have a little one to think about. I had to get it right for him, especially since his father was dead. Looking at Sasha's and Nevaeh's texts, I realized how blessed I was to have two friends who looked out for me like them. I had been in this bed crying and feeling sorry for myself for a few weeks now, but they really held it down. They took care of KJ, cooked and brought me food, cleaned up in the house, and listened to me whine and cry. I will not feel sorry for myself anymore though. What was done was done. KJ is gone and I didn't know why he played me and Alona, but you know what? We will never know. It's not like he is coming back to tell us. I didn't apologize to the girl, but I probably should since I want our kids to have a relationship. I had to be mature and stop worrying about a young love I once had. I see that now. Too bad it caused me to lose a new love, one with someone who was always there-even when I was young. I had just never noticed him. The real him. I guess I didn't know how to look past his circumstances. He was just a kid I felt sorry for at first, then he was just a friend.

Missing Tavian, I looked at my phone and pulled up the picture we took last month when we took KJ to the park. I had never seen my son that happy. I messed that up for us but I was going to try and fix it. Once I got myself together, Tavian may forgive me. Pressing the side button, my screen saver went black. I jumped up and put on some music so I could clean this house top to bottom. I started upstairs and changed the sheets and comforters on the beds, dusted, and then ran the vacuum upstairs. I got the vinegar and baking soda and began scrubbing the bathtub, sink, and toilet. I opened up new air fresheners, put away clean clothes, and sprayed some fabreeze as a final touch. Making my way downstairs and humming some kid's song KJ is always singing about a bumble bee, I scrubbed counters, my glass dining room table, the fridge, and my half bath. I was able to quickly finish up down there since I had not really left my room the past few weeks.

Thank God Neveah had been staying here. I still felt terrible that we hadn't realized she was homeless and that she had no family. I couldn't imagine life without my mom-even though she is still in Jamaica-or my crazy ass brother. Neveah told me she spends holidays alone and birthdays alone. I told her we are her family now so she wouldn't be doing that anymore. As a matter of fact, I know her twentieth birthday is in August so I was going to plan something nice for her. I needed to speak to Covey about it because I think he has a soft spot for my home girl even though he be trying to act like he can't stand her.

For whatever reason, I like glass stuff compared to wood and I had a lot of it in my house. Treajure is always fucking with me and saying she couldn't buy glass if she wanted to because of the twins, but I told her they'd do just fine with the glass in my house as does KJ. That is why he has no toys in any of the rooms with glass. His play room is all tricked out in plastic colorful stuff.

Running up the stairs and taking a deep breathe, all I could smell was air freshener, pine sol, and bleach. That was just what I wanted. I looked in my dresser and took out a white and pink, off the shoulder crop top, dark blue jean shorts, and some white sandals. I then grabbed my pink and white Coach Wristlet and keys. I jumped in the car to go across town and register for classes. I was going to surprise the girls and just show up to school in the fall. As soon as I pulled up to the school, I felt nervous and began to doubt myself. I made myself go to the registrar's office and submit my paperwork. The whole time I was waiting on the old white guy to put everything in the system, I thought about walking out but then I pictured my son's face and realized that I needed to go through with this. Finally, he was finished and handed me the papers I'd come for. Walking out with a fall schedule in my hand, I made my way to the hair shop on Dewey. I had both girls coming in to get their hair done then a couple of regular clients I missed while I spent all that time feeling sorry for myself.

"Well, look who decided to join us, the fairy princess Sasha," exclaimed my cousin Ray using his hands to help him talk and rolling his hips while whipping his head. Even though he was gay, my cousin was cute and funny as a bitch.

"Ok Ray, I am here and since I am a princess, I want my fucking red carpet," I replied. "Who is first?" I asked Navaeh and Treajure.

"Girl, just start us both. I need a perm and you already know Miss Thing here wants to get her hair cut again, shorter this time," Treajure spoke for both of them. Sitting them in the chair and throwing perm in both of their heads, my girls and I spent time laughing and fucking around. The day was just chill. Ray had like four clients all at once and his assistant was looking crazy running around washing heads and removing rollers.

Noticing the brown skin girl who'd just got some fresh tracks glued in stand up from under the dryer and hug up who I guess she thought was her man, I noticed that another client was eyeing the dark skin guy with dreads hard as a bitch. As the two of them walked out after paying Ray, the other girl jumped up as soon as the last crochet twist was in and settled on her head. Throwing Ray his money, she ran out the door after the couple. We heard a commotion so we all went to the window and looked. Damn, it was hair all in the street. Black tracks from the brown skin girl, and brown and blond twists from the big girl. Watching Ray run outside, I had to go see what his crazy ass was talking about.

"Alright ladies, I can see some ass whooping has taken place and hair will need to be repaired. For the right price, I will squeeze you both back in and fix you right up." My cousin spun on his heels in Prada sneakers and twitched his ass back into the shop where we all fell out laughing.

"Ray you ain't shit." I laughed at him holding my stomach laughing. When I'd finished the girls hair, I had to work for a few more hours so I told them I would be at the house soon to pick up KJ and we could have a movie night if they wanted. I looked at my phone as it rang again and was becoming annoyed at the random calls from private and different numbers. It always turned out to be Ajay. I wondered if he know his secret was out. If I hadn't thought he was insane, I would let him know his sister ratted him out and all of his deepest secrets were mine to keep. Getting annoyed, I pressed the answer button roughly with my index finger.

"What Ajay?" I yelled into the phone.

"Sasha, I have been trying to call you for weeks baby. Come on, let's talk about this. Let's work it out," he begged into the phone like the bitch he was.

I'd decided I wanted to get some answers as to how he could pretend with me for this long so I responded, "Ok, Ajay. I will come see you and give you a chance to explain things to me. I will be by there after work."

Chapter 15

Covey

Looking at my boys, I didn't even want to get into all the bullshit in my life, but I knew they wanted to know what's up, so I had to tell them something. This is what I didn't want to happen. I didn't want a female to be the reason I was distracted from finding out who killed Kaneil, or take my focus off of the money I was making in these streets. If I fuck up the money, the whole family gets fucked up. That is the messed up part of being the oldest. All the responsibility falls on me. Don't get me wrong, Jyion helps out and holds his own, but I'd been taking care of my mom's and Sasha long before he was around and now it was all I knew. I leaned back in the leather chair and ran my hands over my face and sighed.

"See, this is why I didn't want to get involved with any female on a serious level. I ain't shit and I know it when it comes to women, and now I fucked up and hurt Neveah. After all she been through at the hands of her parents and that punk ass Frank, I never wanted that shit to happen. I can still picture her face when she seen me and Chanel in the mall. Even then she held her own. Man, she never acted a fool or nothing. She just said hello to me and smiled. I could tell she was hurt but she kept it classy. Then Frank showed up and Chanel started acting up calling her names, and shit got way out of hand."

"Wait, you talking about the girl you was calling thot? I thought she was a whore or something the way you talked about her. I only seen her once at Treajure's spot. She seemed quiet but you know what they say about the quiet ones. I was about to tell Treajure to not have her hanging around my kids," Jyion said.

"Man, I was just calling her that shit, you know how I am. She is a good girl. You know that nigga Frank from over Ghost Town? The fat one with the red Lexus? That was her man for a long time, but he really treated her bad. Anyway, the worst part about the whole situation is I started to fuck with shawty and then when she seen me and Chanel, I never came to help her with Frank's bullshit. I just grabbed up Chanel and left her standing there, letting Chanel call her a bitch and a whore."

"Damn, man. You could have done better than that. You are a real ladies man. Do all the women in the world a favor. Don't try and settle down with one of them because it will definitely end badly. You know a woman scorned and all of that shit," Tavian joked. It looked strange watching him laugh. His usually straight face was all turned up in a smile. I wondered if my sister had something to do with that. I didn't care if he was team Sasha shit, at least I knew she would be taken care of with him. I knew a lot of people thought I didn't want Kaneil to mess with her because she was young, or because he was my friend. Naw, I just knew he was a damn gallis. He was a young pretty boy fucking all the girls and I knew she had no idea. Even from the grave this nigga was breaking her heart again and again.

"Cuz, listen to Tav. Man, these hoes be wilding when they don't get what they want or you leave them for better. Scorned is not the word. I am going through it with this bitch Tauni. She stole some money, but lucky for her I found that shit then she tried to take me into Canada on purpose. And, I found out she had some kids already. I am trying to figure out why they don't live with her before I let her ass take care of mine," Jyion said while shaking his head like he was talking to a slow child.

"So, now we have to figure this shit out with motherfucking Ajay. I never would have thought him of all people was the one coming for us all this time. He killed Kaneil, he tried to rape Treajure, then he started fucking with Sasha." I could see both men's jaws clench in anger when I mentioned the women they loved. "I just don't understand all of this because he had some obsession with Treajure? Where they do that shit at?" Shaking my head, I really didn't know how this shit had happened. I mean, who expects some dude to be stalking a girl since they were kids?

"I think first of all, we should kill his sister. What's that bitch's name? Alona, that's it. We should torture Alona then send him pieces of her body one by one. Then we find anyone else he cares about and do the same. After that, we go after him, or we can just kill this dude right away and worry about this new connect we working with. I don't trust the Mexicans, but the prices are so much better."

"Tav I don't trust them cats either, but we have to make this move. I got a lot of shit I am trying to do right now and I need my funds to line up in a certain way to make that happen. So we meet with them on Sunday to make arrangements for the first shipment. Jyion, I want all of us to be there in case shit goes to the left, and Tavian remember we can't just go around killing people like it's the Wild Wild West. We gonna have enough war play once Jones finds out we are done fucking with him. When I went and picked up the last shipment, I tried to talk to him about the problems with the pricing and the weed shipment from Cali and he brushed me off, so fuck him."

"Man look, I got two kids and two on the way so you already know I ain't playing no fucking games man. I never came to America to be broke. I am going hard for mine," Jyion said all hyped up.

"Wait nigga, did you say two kids on the way? Yo', all this bread you stacking you need to invest in some condoms or plastic wrap, something. I guess I have to hurry up and get a little one to catch up to yo' ass," I said in shock for real because this dude breeds a girl as he looks at her.

After we set up everything for Sunday and kicked it for a while longer, I left to go to my crib. I had tried to call Nevaeh. I wanted to go hang out with her but she sent me to voicemail. Calling her back, she finally answered on the third ring.

"What the fuck you doing that you can't answer your phone when I am calling?" I questioned.

"Covey, I don't have to answer you. I am not shit to you. I am not doing a thing but studying. I sent you to voicemail because I don't want to talk. I am good over here so please leave me alone," she said in an exasperated tone like she was talking to a small child or some shit.

"Yeah, you good over there, then why did you end up answering. You miss the kid huh?"

"I answered after the third time in case it was an emergency. I mean, shit, I started caring about you and in your line of business anything can happen so I wanted to make sure you was safe. Now that I know you're good, please get off my line," she said just shutting me all the way down. I am not about to beg a girl, so fuck it.

"Aight cool, take care Nevaeh," I told her before hanging up the phone. Maybe she will call me back, and if she doesn't, fuck it I thought in the back of my mind. Even though I wanted to check my phone for missed calls, I just continued to drive.

Riding by the place I knew Frank hung out, I didn't see him on the block.

"Hey yo', where Frank at?" I called out to a group of kids playing basketball in the middle of the road." No one bothered to respond except one of the older boys with some purple shorts that looked too small on him and a ripped up shirt.

"Frank is in the back of that brick house smoking a blunt. That's his place so he should still be there because his whip is in the driveway and he is alone," he spoke in a low tone.

Handing him a hundred dollar bill, he grabbed a little boy that looked to be as poor as him and they made their way to the corner store.

"Come on Junior we can go eat now. Hurry and I will find a way to buy you a pair of shoes too," I heard him say to what had to be his little brother. Looking down I realized the smaller boy had on some flip flops that where way too big and looked like they had seen better days. Damn man that reminded me of Sasha and me when we were coming up. All I wanted to do was make sure she was straight and not suffering.

"Yo' little man, hold up. Y'all come here for a minute," I called out to them.

"Sir, do you need something else?" the older boy asked.

"Yeah, meet me inside the villa over there," I pointed to the plaza up the road on Lyell. "I'ma be there in a few minutes. Just go up there and wait. I got you, so don't leave." Nodding their head both boys ran up the street.

Parking and jumping out of my whip I made my way to the back of Frank's house. Seeing him sitting there on the phone laughing it up with some bitch rubbing on his fat belly and smoking a blunt, I felt disgusted. This nigga didn't even have on a shirt. Walking behind him I grabbed him in a choke hold.

When She's Your Everything

I made sure he seen my face before I took out my knife and flicked it open. Pointing the blade to the tip of his neck I could see the fear in his face. His Samsung phone fell from his hands as they began to shake and shattered on the ground.

Leaning down and whispering in his ear, "This is for Nevaeh". I slowly took the knife and eased it from one ear to the other. I waited a few minutes watching the blood drip as his fat body fell back on the concrete steps. Using his shirt to wipe the knife off, I put it back in my pocket and went a few backyards down. Exiting from a neighbor's yard I walked to my car and made my way to The Villa.

As soon as I walked up the boys where standing outside waiting on me.

"Yo' why y'all not inside the store?" I asked opening the door and letting them go in before me. "The guy told us to leave because we look like we are going to steal something and he knows we can't afford anything," he said, looking down in shame. "What's your name?" I asked him pissed that some adults could be so cold hearted. I guess I get it though. He didn't look like he had any money, but you shouldn't judge a book by its cover.

"My name is Antwan and my little brother's name is Duke," he introduced himself. "Aight I am Covey, let's get you little niggas some kicks." I made sure to show out in the store since they felt the kids couldn't afford shit up in there. I copped them each three pair of Jordan's and some Timbs. I don't think I have ever seen a kid smile so much. The oldest couldn't have been more than ten years old. I wonder where their parents were. They really should be having someone look out for them better. When they had their shoe bags in hand we made our way over to Rainbow next door and I let them get some new clothes too. All together I dropped less than a rack and made these kids day. I be spending more than that on sneakers sometimes, I gotta do better. Helping them made me think about Nevaeh. I wish she would let me help her more when she got in her place. At least she let me cop her some furniture and food. I paid six months of her rent too but she didn't figure that out yet or she would be cussing me out.

"Aight boys, I gotta get out of here but I'ma drop you guys off so hop in." I rolled through the Lil Cesears drive through and grabbed them some pizza and wings before we got to their place. Pulling up to the address on Whitney Street I couldn't believe the condition of the spot they were living in. The apartment building would probably be condemned soon because that happens all the time in this neighborhood. "I want you guys to stay out of trouble, read a book or something but no hanging out at night and shit. I'ma send someone around here to look out for you guys and I will roll back through when I can."

"Thank you Covey." they both said dapping me up and running up to their door with all their new stuff, still smiling.

Driving home I felt good about today. I knew I had to get rid of Frank after what he did and I looked out for two kids. I just wish I could see Nevaeh and hold her in my arms. Walking in my house and looking around the kitchen, I realized I was lonely. I never bring these females to my house, and if I go to them I am only there to fuck and leave. When Nevaeh was here, I was happy. I can't believe she had me playing games like I was a kid. Opening the door the my room I thought my mind was playing tricks because there was someone in my bed. My heart starting racing as I pulled my nine out of my back, I am hoping for some reason that it was Nevaeh but if she was here she would have cooked and it would have smelled like her.

Turning on the lights Chanel's ass jumped up naked as the day she was born.

"Arghhhh, babe it's me. Don't shoot!" she yelled.

"Chanel what the fuck are you doing in my house?" I put the gun away and snatched her clean out the bed. I have an alarm system so I am not sure how she got in here. Before I could open the front door and throw her out, the bell rang,

"Covey, I need to talk to you," came Nevaeh's voice from the other side of the door.   "Shit".

Chapter 16

Ajay

Man fuck. Messing with this amazon looking bitch caused me to lose the only women I had ever loved. I know now that Sasha is done with me I will never get close to Treajure again. Treajure is like a drug that I couldn't live without. I can still remember what her body felt like when we were young and I was so close to being the first to sample her goods. Until that fuck boy Jyion interrupted what I was doing. My homeboy Mel was killed over that shit but I was not sad at his life being taken because I saw him looking at Treajure's exposed body and I knew he was going to try and fuck her, but she belongs to me.

Leaving thoughts of the past behind, I looked over at her ass all balled up in my tan leather Infiniti seats and I couldn't help but mug her ass. I told this fucking girl get rid of the baby. First of all, I knew she was trying to trap me with a baby a long time ago so I was extra careful but somehow she got me drunk on the right day which I am sure she had all planned out, and next thing you know she is screaming pregnant. She probably froze my sperm and used a turkey baster to shove it back in her pussy once it was defrosted. I seen that shit on an episode of the Game before and I know these bitches be trying everything.

Calling Sasha for the hundredth time with my right hand while driving with my left, I could see that Bionca wanted to fucking say something. But if she knows what is good for her ugly ass then she will keep those dick suckers closed. Every time I get sent to Sasha's voicemail, I can feel my temper raise one more notch. I am surprised my fucking head isn't on fire, this bitch better answer her fucking phone. I am not giving up on her and after I seen her and that dude with the scar on his face having lunch the other day I knew she called herself being serious about moving on, and I am not having that at all.

Yeah, I know I am doing Bionca's ass wrong and sound like a fuck nigga but I never told her she was my girl. She just began assuming shit. I would think that all this time she would have gotten the hint. I don't take her ass nowhere in public. I fuck her with all the lights off and sometimes I shove a pillow over her face just so I can bust and the rest of the time its face down ass up just so I can get a fuck. I met this broad at a corner store a few years ago when I first hit the town and I needed a place to stay until I figured out how to get my money right. I was living with my sister at the time but I was so tired of listening to her cry about her punk ass baby father's death, I had to get out of there before she was next. I needed a quick come up so I could be ready to get Sasha and that is just what I did.

If you hear Bionca tell it, we were a couple and I up and left her for Sasha. When I stayed in her crib I slept in a whole other room and would bring chicks to the house all the time, smash and all. I never paid a bill or bought any food, not even a grape, but I expected ole girl to make sure my meals were ready daily. Shit, she is one of those under confident type of girls who will do anything just to feel wanted by a nigga. Yeah, I fucked her out of convenience but not because we had anything going on. Now I am going to have to kiss her ass a little so she doesn't run her mouth and tell Sasha any fucking thing else. Who would have thought she really had the nerve to video tape us fucking and then sent the shit to my girl? Thinking about this shit pissed me off all over again. Pulling over a few blocks from the hospital, I hit the locks on the door.

"Yo', get the fuck out man. I gotta try and go fix this shit wit' wifey." I reached over her and opened the door so she could walk her ass the rest of the way home. Sitting there rubbing her stomach and silently crying, I guess she thought I was gonna give a fuck. "Bionca, are you deaf? GET THE FUCK OUT!!" I yelled. Slowly she got her awkward looking ass out of the car and turned around to talk shit.

"You are so heartless Ajay. Who treats the mother of their only child like this. Yeah, I said only child because Sasha's son is by Kaneil and you will never have a baby with her." She laughed slamming my door. All I could see is red, throwing the car in park I jumped out and ran around the front grabbing her wobbly ass by the fake ass red hair she had in.

"Bitch, don't say Sasha's name ever. Fuck you and that baby I told you not to try and fucking have. I been nice to you, as nice as I can be. I never really told you how I felt because I was sparing your feelings, but you gross me out. That's why I don't fuck wit' you like that. You always hitting my line begging me to come and fuck you, you can barely keep a job, and you are not wife material. I don't give a fuck about your pussy being all over the internet or you being pregnant. Stay the fuck away from me, and I mean it."

Kicking her in the back and side a few times I left her lying on the sidewalk as I strolled to my whip. Once I got in I never looked back, peeling away from the curb I made my way to the house me and Sasha used to share. If I can just talk to her face to face I am sure I can fix this and once I fixed this shit I will go check on Bionca and our baby. I mean the kid is here now so I have to just roll with it. As soon as I pulled up to the house Sasha lived in, I noticed some cut up and bleached clothes out on the front of the street. I knew it was my shit right away but I didn't care. I had more clothes at home and I deserved that. Sasha's car wasn't there but maybe she had someone pick it up so I would think she is not home.

Banging on the door, I tried calling her at the same time. I didn't hear any movement from inside and she was sending me straight to voicemail. Damn, hoping up the front stairs I decided to try my key. As soon as I looked at the lock I could tell it as changed, this one was shiny and gold the one before was silver and scuffed up. Damn it man, I don't even have anyone to call to help me win Sasha back over. I can't tell people the real reason why I want to be with her so badly. My mother and sister know about my obsession with Treajure and look what I had to do to my own mother. I learned to keep my true intentions to myself at all costs after that, I don't know why people can't understand what it's like to want someone. I can't help the woman I want doesn't know I exist. She will someday and when she does, I will live out all of the scenarios I have been playing over and over again in my mind, only this time they will be real.

Getting in my car, I peeled off the street. I didn't put my hands on Sasha nothing and see how she is treating me. These women are no good, you treat them a little better than what they are and they get in their feelings for every little thing. Dialing one on my phone again I decided to leave a voicemail.

"Sasha, I am getting tired of this little temper tantrum you are having, Ok yeah, I messed around with this girl, I knew her before I hooked up with you so it's not a big fucking deal so stop making it one. I am ready to come home and get my dick wet. I'm handling some business and then I will be at the house so you better fucking be there and have my key for the new lock."

Pulling up to Strong Hospital I parked in the garage and made my way to labor and delivery. As soon as I walked onto the floor a lot of the nurses and other female staff were looking my way and pointing, whispering and some where even flirting. What the fuck is going on? I prayed this dumbass girl did not do no stupid shit like tell these people I beat her up or nothing like that.

Chapter 17

Bionca

Lying in this hospital bed and looking over at Ajay as he sits next to me with his head in his hands and shoulders slumped I know he has to go soon. He will never straighten up and will always treat me as second best. He is not looking like his puppy got ran over because of me and our baby he is in his feelings because he is going to lose his "girl". You want to know the fucked up shit, I was his girl or so I thought. I was here before I ever heard of a fucking Sasha. He was promising me the world, living with me then all the sudden he needed his own space and he didn't want a baby by me. This was not our first pregnancy scare; I had to work hard to get this baby with him. Once we had sex and he forgot a condom, the next day he beat my door in and forced me to take the morning after pill. So this time I made sure to plan this one out and then go out of town until I was at least three months pregnant. I remember thinking he would be happy about our child eventually, that this baby would bring us closer but if anything it tore us apart. He stopped having sex with me and he barely comes around, only once in a while for me to top him off. He has not bought our baby a pamper or a onesie nothing.

Ever since I found out about Sasha it'd been nothing but him telling me how over they are and how she is still in love with her dead ex-boyfriend, the one I think he helped have killed. See I pay attention when he is on the phone with his friends and I check his phones. On the real I wouldn't put shit over on this nigga. It was all lies with this fuck nigga, he just comes around when he wants to do freaky shit that I know Sasha is not doing. Stuff like him fucking me in the ass and letting him cum in my mouth. It's all good. He and his little bitch are going to pay at this point. She fractured my ribs, broke my leg, and did some damage to my back and shoulder with that crow bar. Thank God the nurses and doctors said the baby will be ok but I will need to be on bedrest and they want me there until the baby is born. They basically told me all the pain I am in means my baby will probably experience distress so they are making me have her within the next twenty-four hours.

Watching the nurse come in and move around doing whatever the fuck she is supposed to be doing I seen her look at me oddly at first. I hope it is not another bitch that Ajay's been sticking his community dick in. After she came in, another nurse came in and pretended to check my IV but was laughing at me the whole time. What the fuck is going on here. Is there shit on my face, did something funny happen and I missed it, maybe it is because of the scrapes and cuts on my face from his crazy ass girlfriend. Getting up and slowly creeping to the door, I cracked it opened and saw a group of staff members looking at someone holding a phone and everyone was laughing except a dark skin girl with a kind face and short dreads. The first nurse that came in to my room was all hyped up and pointing to the phone.

"Yes, she is my patient. the girl in the video." What the fuck is she talking about, girl in a video? I have never been on TV so I am confused and I know that hoe is talking about me because she shifted her eyes to my door when she said that.

"Yo', I am outta here for now. Let me know when they release you and I will give you a ride," Ajay said as he brushed past me and left the room. He never even helped me back into the bed or asked if I needed anything. I guess that meant he was not going to be here when I had our daughter. I am having my baby a few weeks early because of him and his nonsense. You know what? Fuck him. I got a surprise for his ass when I am out of here. Seeing the girl with the dreads come in a few hours later after I called for a blanket, I was happy to see her and not the others. The ones who I am sure were laughing at me and were barely doing their job.

"How are you doing? Well, I guess that's a stupid question since you are in here. But thank God your little blessing is strong and doing good," she chatted away while fluffing my pillows and covering me with the second blanket that she had heated up. I will be sure to leave her supervisor a compliment for her. Reading her tag, I noticed her name is Cindy.

"Cindy, is there something wrong with my face? I didn't look in the mirror when I came in I was very concerned for my child but I did notice a lot of the staff looking at me and laughing," I asked her hoping she would tell me what the fuck is going on and why I am being laughed at like I am the joke on the bubble gum wrapper. Seeing Nurse Cindy hesitate and look around the room, she walked closer to the bed.

"Look sweetie, I don't know you personally and I don't judge people. What you chose to do in your private life is not my business but in case you didn't know, it has become the public's business." Holding up her phone she handed it to me. I accepted it with shaking hands and saw a video ready to play. As soon as I hit play, there I was on the screen with Ajay's dick in my mouth. Watching for a few more minutes I realized it was the full video I'd sent to Ajay's phone hoping that Sasha would see it.

Handing the nurse her phone back I thanked her and rolled over on my side. I could tell she wanted to say something else. I could see her shadow as she stood there for a few minutes hesitating, thinking of something to reassure me or make me feel better. How can I feel better when my secrets are now all over the internet? If this shit was on Facebook, then that means it was on YouTube, Snap Chat, and anywhere else someone could watch a video. I guess I played myself, I sent the video first. Hearing the shuffling of Cindy's shoes as she made her way to the door, she shut it. I rolled over and cried. I cried for the love I kept trying to find with a man who clearly didn't love me. I cried for the days and nights I spent as a child hating myself because I had parents who didn't love me. And I cried for the unborn baby that I am carrying who will not know love from me because I don't know how to give what I have never received.

I woke up in so much pain I could not scream or move. My stomach was in knots and I kept feeling sharp pains, like little electric shocks. Sitting up as much as I could, that is when I noticed all the blood. It was everywhere on the bed. Hitting the call button for the nurse, I picked up my phone and bypassed all the messages from so-called friends wanting info on my video and any other gossip they could dig up. I dealed Ajay's number but he never answered. I was only after eleven at night so I know he was not sleeping. Not even bothering to leave a message, I tried to breathe as the nurses ran in the room.

"Ok honey, lay back. This is not what we planned but the baby is coming now. She is in distress. Do you hear her heartbeat going crazy?" she asked me. I nodded yes. I was scared. I didn't want Ajay's baby to die. It was a part of him and me, an important part. Before I could ask a question they were pulling stuff out of the wall and snatching my IV bag off the pole and attaching it to the bed.

"CODE BLUE!" they began yelling while wheeling me down the hallway.

I woke up a few hours later in even more pain. Running my hands down my belly, I could feel something sharp and metal sticking out of me right above my pelvic bone. I guess I had a C-section. I really don't know what happened.

"Hello Bionca. Can you tell me where you are?" a doctor walked over and asked me.

"I think I am in Strong hospital," I replied, unsure of where I was for sure. I felt disoriented and confused.

"Yes you are, we had to give you an emergency C-section due to the complications from your accident earlier in the day. Your daughter is doing fine and you can see her whenever you are ready," she said with a smile on her face.

They tried to get me to hold my daughter the full three days I was there, but I declined. If her daddy wasn't coming to see her and be with us, it was a waste of time having her. I named her Ajayanna after her father. I called him every hour on the hour until it was time for me to be released. I never received a call or a text back, nothing. I had to have my sister Tamara come and pick me up after she got the car seat from my house. I had never felt so depressed in my life.

Listening to my daughter scream and watching her tiny face turn beet red, I just wanted to throw her out of the window or put this blanket over her face to shut her up. I couldn't believe I was stuck with this crying ass baby. The only thing stopping me from hurting her is the fact that her face looks just like the man I am in love with, and I couldn't hurt him. I had been dealing with this all on my own day and night for a week now, and I am fed up.

If Ajay didn't want to come see us, I would take his daughter to go see him. I was still dealing with people calling me about the video that was online. I was fired from my job at Frontier Communications as a team lead because somehow the video made it to my LinkedIn account. How do you get fired while on maternity leave? That's ok. That can take that shit up with unemployment because I was going to make sure to collect on they punk asses. I should file a lawsuit. Maybe Ajay can help me find a lawyer. One I win, we can take the money and move away and then he will be all mine. He won't have to deal with Sasha anymore or be in the streets.

Feeling a little better, I grabbed the baby and fed her, then burped her the way I saw my sisters do with their babies. Once she stopped crying, she kind of smiled up at me with her pretty eyes. She has her father's dark coloring and my brown eyes oval shaped eyes. Giving her a quick sponge bath I found a pretty pink and white outfit to put on her. The top was white with pink polka dots and some little white satin slippers. Securing her in the baby car seat I took a fast shower and threw on some all-black leggings and a white and black striped shirt that said *ON FLEEK*. I had some all red box braids in my hair that I pinned up and when I looked in the mirror, I was feeling myself. Yeah, I am kind of tall for a female. I am about five foot eleven and I have wide feet. My body shape is not ideal but I am not ugly. Every girl cannot be a perfect size seven.

Jumping in the car I was singing Beyonce's *Hold Up* and thinking of all the ways Ajay can make shit up to me. As soon as I pulled up and parked, his front door opened. But instead of Ajay coming out, it was Sasha. It's always Sasha, he changed his phone number on me and our daughter but she is over there chilling like I just didn't have a baby and they didn't ruin my fucking life. Slamming the door, I snatched the baby carrier and ran up the stairs to bang on the door.

"Sasha baby, I knew you would be back," he said, opening the door. "Oh Bionca. What are you doing here? I know I told you don't come to my house unless it's an emergency?" he said with a disgusted look on his face.

"So, seeing your daughter is not a priority? Me having an emergency surgery because she could have died is not an emergency?" I began yelling.

I guess he decided to let me in so the neighbors didn't get start looking with all the screaming and hand clapping I was doing. Since I know he keeps drugs and guns in his house this was the smartest decision he could have made.

"Let me see her yo'," he asked, snatching Ajayanna from me and taking her out of her seat. After he played with her for a little while she fell asleep and he put her back in her car seat. "So you can fuck or naw?" he asked me, rubbing his hand on my thighs.

"I am still bleeding," I told him, sadly. He began taking his big dick out and stroking it. He pulled me to the bedroom in the back not even looking back at our baby. Standing me on the edge of the bed he put pressure on my shoulders making me sit down.

"Come on, open up. You know what I want, girl," he said on a moan as he shoved his dick in my mouth. Not even giving me a chance to respond, or spit on his dick, nothing, he was ramming himself in and out of my mouth. Feeling him grab the back of my head I knew what was coming next. "Bionca, you better not spit my shit out" he said in a cold tone as he let his hot cum fill my mouth and my throat. I had no choice but to swallow as much as I could. "Lick it up, baby" he said as he used the tip to rub it over my tongue and all over my face.

Feeling degraded, I just sat there with cum running down my chin. I looked up to see him laughing. How could he be so cruel, so mean to me and I loved him? I did everything for him when he got here. I fed him, clothed him, and even gave him all of my money.

"Aight, well thanks for that and for bringing the little one through. I will holla at you later." With that said, he turned around to take off his clothes. I guess he wanted to get in the shower or something. I could feel all these years of being overlooked by him turn into rage and in that last second, instead of turning around to walk out of the door, I turned to the left and grabbed the worn yellow baseball bat he had leaning up against the door and whacked him in the back of his head. He fell to the ground with a thud. I calmly grabbed him and rolled him onto the bed. I could feel my staples from my C-section pulling so I used the bat to leverage him and roll him again.

Once he was in the middle of the bed, I ran and grabbed the lighter fluid he had by the back door and the matches on the counter. This motherfucker wants to keep playing me. Well, he can play himself in hell. Pouring the lighter fluid on him and the blankets, I threw two matches onto the bed and watched the flames start to bloom. Laughing, I made my way to the front of the house. Hearing the baby crying again, I decided to cut my losses and leave her to rot with her father. She failed her mission which was for me to get my man. As I climbed in my old blue Honda, I noticed Sasha's BMW whip into the driveway. The flames where not yet visible to the outside so when she ran in the house I was hoping she would also perish in the fire. Instead, she came out clutching her purse and my baby. Who told this bitch to save my baby?

Before I could react, the police and fire department pulled up and began putting out the fire and speaking to Sasha. When the EMT's began working on the baby, I decided to do the only thing I could.

"Oh my God! My baby! Is she ok?" I sobbed running over to the officer who was closest. "Ma'am, is this your child?" the officer asked me with a question mark written on his face.

"Yes sir, this is my daughter and that women kidnapped her. I believe she also set my boyfriend's house on fire. Officer, where is my boyfriend? AJAY!" I screamed and carried on putting on a show and while I climbed in the ambulance with my daughter, I watched the officers with a smile as they put handcuffs on a screaming Sasha, who I imagine is now being booked for kidnapping and murder.

To Be Continued...

Text Shan to 22828 to stay up to date with new releases, sneak peeks, contest, and more...

Check your spam if you don't receive an email thanking you for signing up.

Text SPROMANCE to 22828 to stay up to date on new releases, plus get information on contest, sneak peeks, and more!

CPSIA information can be obtained
at www.ICGtesting.com
Printed in the USA
LVOW12s1739081016

507970LV00018B/357/P